OTARD

OTARD

Extra Old

Lawrence Qua CC

PARTRIDGE

To order additional copies of this book, contact
Toll Free 800 101 2657 (Singapore)
Toll Free 1 800 81 7340 (Malaysia)
orders.singapore@partridgepublishing.com

www.partridgepublishing.com/singapore

CONTENTS

Chapter 1

In the Beginning

He is a Capricorn. He was born in January. His star reads he had a weak knee and he fell down lots of times, and suffering bruised in his knee cap in his childhood days. He fell not because he is suffering from weak knees but was kicked of his bicycle by his close friend, and was pushed to the ground by his friend. His star said he is a leader and will climbed the ladder to the top. He will be successful. Never the less he is a goat, a mountain goat. But no body thought that he would be a scapegoat. How do you feel, being a scapegoat? Do you like being a scapegoat? What is a scapegoat, you may ask?

The Longman Dictionary of Contemporary English gives the definition as someone who is blame for something that happens, even if it is not his fault. It is horrible isn't it to be blame for something you never do or said. To be labeled as a mad man in love with all the women in the world. This is insane, you may say. This was what he had to faced, as he was called God. Not only is he blamed for the love relationships, of married couples, and the birth of their children, he is also blamed for the activity in the world affairs. They wanted his blood as a sacrificial lamb, for their nations of the world. He do not gain a single cent from the title of godhead, only problems, and troubles, and more troubles. He spend his own monies to fulfill their wishes of the people who called him God. The people who called him God, wanted more and more till he reached a state where he had no more to spend, and also lost his employment. His property was destroyed and his marriage to his wife dissolved. He lost his two daughters. This let him to dislodge the tangle he got himself in his birth, after he lost all he have. They disallow him to make offerings to Gods or to attend to any faith at the time of Christ Kingdom. No one would believe such a story but is true. This is his life. This is what happens.

What is said is said, and what is done is done. It is remembered. It is kept in the mind. The mistake we make in our mind still remains although the past is already gone. The Mind is everything. What is not in the conscious to-day is in the subconscious or buried in the depth of the unconscious. The mind is a plane of thoughts shared by the people of the world. Those with mental telepathic powers can tap on the thoughts of others while others who are not capable are influenced by these thoughts projection through daily thinking. These thoughts projectionist can be sorcerers, warlocks and witches. The will tell you how to eat? how to work? and how to wear clothes. They are in the brain controlling our daily life. They are the father, mother in the brain. This is a story of him who is called God by those in West and the East that practiced thoughts projections. They wanted him to speak in the thoughts of individual, and carried out their daily chores, and tell them how to make with their wife and children. They wanted him to represent god. It is unfair to him, for he have to bear the burden of the family, and be an AM driver, that pilot the soul, mastery of the life. All he wanted is to be free.

Otard

In the year near end of 1979, somewhere in England, in a small town, near West Ham Football Stadium a road not far away, a man way burning his properties and belonging. Everything in his house were stripped to emptiness and brought to the garden in the little terrace house in England and set ablaze. The burning took place for near to a week. Furniture, books, collections and various objects and were destroyed in the fire. The burning took place all day and night, till one night a local police constable of the London Police Force called on his house to tell him to put out the blaze. This was the last day of the burning, and he put out the blaze and called it a night and turned in for bed. He, I will refer to as Otard. I call him Otard as I think this name is suitable for this story. I won't use his real name as he has suffered enough, and have lost a lot in his battle with his thoughts. Otard was a young man, in his late 30's. He was a married man with a wife and two beautiful daughters and he loved them very much. His children were at this time around the age of 3 and 5. His eldest daughter aged 5 was named Aniroc and his younger daughter was named Anirbas. Of course this were not their real name. I used nick names to protect their identity. I used only short names to make it easier to relate the story. The children lived a normal live attending nursery and play school within the location of their home. On Week-end Otard will take his children down to Hyde Park to see children fly kites. Otard, like kite flying, as he comes from a country where there is a kite flying season, where children goes out flying kite. A kite is a piece of egg paper pasted on some bamboo sticks, and tied to a string and fly according to the direction of the winds.

His wife Esor, this is of course also not her real name is a short plum woman of build. In her earlier childhood days, she studied ballet dancing, and this was one of the reason, how Otard was attracted to her. He likes ballet dancing his admirer was the famous Margret Fonteyn. Margret Fonteyn is widely regarded a one to the greatest classical dancer of all time. She was born in 1919 and died in 1991. Margret Fonteyn famous dance include Cinderella, Sleeping Beauty, Romeo and Juliet and many others.

Both Otard and Esor came from the East. They were brought up in the Eastern and Oriental Tradition, but were influenced by the teachings, and Western custom. She went over to England to study Nursing. She was there for a couple of years when she met a friend of Otard, who was Anasus. Together, they build a friendship. Anasus was a big size woman, and comes from a wealthy family from Ipoh a small town in Malaysia. Anasus also went there to study Nursing. Her ambition is to become a Matron. They were studying at Popular Hospital, in the East End of London.

Anasus requested her to bring a gift to Otard for Otard's birthday which falls in January. The gift was a wood carving, of a loving couple sitting together and with the word inscribed on it," Me and You, You and Me, that is the way it will always be". She, Esor was returning to Penang for her holidays. She called on Otard's home, to deliver Anasus gift. At this time, she Esor invited him to a party at her house, where they are celebrating the birthday of her brother Nesie. Nesie birthday party took place some days later in Esor parents house. Otard accepted the invitation, and attended the party. Otard, came to the party on his metallic gold colour Honda CB 100. Honda CB 100 is the latest trend of motor cycle at that time. It was all Otard can afford to purchased. Otard came from a poor family. Otard and Esor came to know each other better, in their communication during the party. Esor comes from a well off family. Otard then invited Esor to spent his birthday with him which falls some days later, in the month of January. She accepted. This was the beginning of the Heartache of Otrard by the Numbers

Chapter 2

Love Life

Otard already had a female friend who he has dated for a few years. She was Eel. She was beautiful and slim, a small size, short lady. She was a clerk, at the local smelting firm. She was a senior to Otard and was older than 7 years. Eel comes from a middle class family, some where in the town in Perak. Eel, lives in her sister house. Eel, sister is a married woman, and she lives with her husband and her husband parents. Eel, finds it inconvenient to live with her sister parents. At this time Otard was working in Hotel Malaysia and in his work he found friendship in Notsgnik a fellow room steward who was working there with him. He discussed with Notsgnik the problems of Eel, and her accommodation at her sister's house and need assistance to find a temporary accommodation.

Notsgnik was most helpful. He said, he will discussed with his Mum to see if she could stay at his house. Notsgnik then informed Otard she Eel, can reside at their house. Before Eel, switched accommodation Otard visited her at her sister house, in Jelutong and met her sister's father-in –law. He was Nat. Nat was a nice man, and was very friendly. Otard had a talk with Nat. Nat then played a very lovely record which Otard could never forget the words of the song. The record was "Here's is the Answer" by Skeeter Davis. Otard was a song enthusiast, and from that day on, he was looking for the particular song. Otard broke the good news to Eel, that she can come and lived in his best friend house, at Irving Road. Following this, some days after, she moved to her new accommodation at Irving Road. All this takes place in the small island of Pulau Pinang, off the West coast of Malaysia.

Now Otard found himself have a problem. The problem is How to tell Eel about Esor, his new found friend Esor? His birthday arrived. Esor was supposed to meet Otard at 10.00 am for his birthday so they could spend the day together. Esor was a horrible person. She never turned up for the appointment. Otard waited for her the whole day, and did not go anywhere. She did not even phone to inform of her change of plans. She never turned up till 7.00pm that evening. Otard, was upset and furious at her behavior. When she arrived at Otard house, Otard told her to go home. She refused so Otard took her on his Honda CB100 to her home. She requested to drop her some distance from her house. She said she will walk home. Otard then dropped her at the junction of the road leading to her house. Otard then went straight to find Eel. As usual, Eel was there waiting for him. They spent the time together till 10.30 pm then Otard departs for his home. When he reached home, his step-mother Nae asked him where he had taken Esor. She mentioned Esor parents phone and ask where their daughter were, as it was late. He told her he took Esor home at 7.30pm and that is the last He saw of her. Otard was worried and panicked as he was the last person with her, after her mother dropped her at his step-mother house.

The phone ringed again, this time it was good news, Esor mother Hol, said her daughter has come home. That was the end of the event for the day for Otard. He had enough of Esor foolishness. She Esor was playing with the thoughts of Otard. Otard was contemplating of giving her up, for to him such a girl was nothing but trouble and heartache. The next day came, and she came by Otard home very early. Otard, asked her "What do you want?. Esor does not answer the question put forward by Otard. She said she wanted to commit suicide and went to the beach last night after he rejected her, but changed her mind. Otard, took her back and they tried to be friends. They went out daily, and one day she came by Otard house and his step-mother was not in. Otard was in the Washroom. The wash room was in the kitchen separated by a kitchen door. While he was in the toilet he was shocked and could not believe his vision and it was as if he had third eyes. He saw Esor dipped her hands into her panties and took some droppings from her vagina and stir it into the drink she made for him. When Otard came out of the wash room, he found he could not enter the kitchen where she Esor is. He shouted to her to open the door. She finally opened the kitchen door, and there he found the drink she had made for him. He could not resist the thought and urge to take the drink immediately, which he did.

Otard love for Esor begins that day. He listened to everything she says. It was like magic. Anything they wish can come true. He wanted to leave Malaysia and go far away to the land overseas. Otard had pasted in his scrapbook about London, and how much he liked to lived there. He, Otard was having problems with his step-mother Nae. Nae was complaining to Otard's father that his son Otard is not doing house keeping in the house were Otard reside in. Otard father, Rovivrus wrote to Otard eldest sister Nail and complained. Nail wrote to Otard and complained, of their father wishes. Otard was very angry and frightened of his step-mother, Nae. Nae wanted the house for herself, and wanted Otard out of the way. Otard dream finally came through.

Chapter 3

The Journey to the West

There came an opening overseas, in the United Kingdom. This is the beginning of the journey to the west where all his problems begin. A group personnel recruiting manager from the Center Enterprise came to Pulau Pinang and is looking for people to work in his company hotels in the United Kingdom. He was Nairb. He was from Center Hotels, Ccenter Eenterprises. He Nairb was staying at the Eastern and Oriental Hotel. Nairb friend was the manager of the hotel. He was Ynod. Otard saw this as an opportunity to grasp. He immediately went to see him at the Eastern and Oriental Hotel to grasp the opportunity. There was vacancy for commis waiter. Otard told Nairb, he was interested in the commis waiter vacancy and would like to apply for the position. Nairb told him to write to him, once he returned to England. Otard, did just that and Narib sent him the forms for application for the vacant position. Nairb office and Otard corresponded for a year. The good news finally came, He got the job. Otard immediately broke the news to Esor. Esor was pleased. Esor had to returned to England. She is a State Enrolled Nurse attached to Popular Hospital, in the East End of London.

Before Esor depart, he told Otard to update her with the latest information, and to let her know of his arrival in

England. At the end of Septemper 1974, Otard received a telegram informing him that the positioned he applied for is successful and to go down to the British High Commission in Kuala Lumpur for interview. He also was requested to visit the appointed doctor, Dr Allen and Dr Gutensen for medical check up. Immediately, Otard made his appointment to see Dr Allen and Dr Gutensen. Otard got to get out of the house he lives in in Pulau Pinang, as he was no welcome there. The sooner the better for him. His appointment came, he saw Dr Allen and Dr Gutensen, and had an x –ray. He was then disclosed that one of rib bone in his right rib is broken though is healed and all right now. After all these, in a few days later Otafrd and a friend took a train to the capital, Kuala Lumpur to called at the British High Commission. The interview went out well. Otard and his friend came back to Penang that evening.

Now Otard was all ready to go. It is as if the mind knows his every move. The radio blares out songs like "The Old man in the street of London" and "Leaving on a Jet Plane". This made Otard feel more excited about his trip to England. The news paper came out with colored pictures of London, which he cut out and pasted in his scrap book. He was all excited. He inform Esor of the finalization of the situation. He breaks the news to Eel, telling her if he do not return in two years he is to married another man of her choice and wishes. He did not tell her he was going to live with Esor once he arrived in London. Otard told no one of this. At this time Otard was working in Hotel Malaysia, and one of the room guest was kind enough to write a letter of introduction to his friend in Essex introducing Otard. The work permit for Otard to work in the United Kingdom was for a hotel in Essex. The room guest was Nhoj and he was a race horse trainer. The girl Otard was supposed to meet in Essex is Nna. Otard was supposed to work in Essex according to his work permit. He sold his motor cycle Honda CB 100 to his work colleague. With this cash he was able to purchase an air ticket to London. Another of his work colleague Mil, was in the process of setting up a travel Bureau. Otard requested Mil to help him get the air ticket. Mil help Otard acquired the ticket at around RM 800.00. It was a Union D'Transport Airlines flight, that takes off from Singapore and transit at D'Gaule Air Port in France. There he had to catch an air France to United Kingdom, arriving at Heathrow Airport, London. Otard was pleased with all the help he could get.

Hi friends advised him to buy some gold chain to take along with him for financial security which could be redeemed for money in an emergency. He purchased one Gold chain from Cheong Yoon Gold Smith from down town Penang. He also purchased a talisman casing in which he purchased a jade blade and insert in into a gold casing wearing it as his enchanted amulet. Penang is famous for its gold market. He purchased a Samsonite Suit Case. He bought that suit case as it advertised on television that an elephant sat of it and is still intact. He was now ever ready. Otard wrote to Esor as he finalized with the trip to United Kingdom and the arrival time. He seek the help of his friend from the German Class, where they study German together, to transport him to airport. His friend Gnoy agreed, and the big day was set. Gnoy was to collect Otard from his house, together with his father and step-mother and his step-sister to the Pulau Pinang Bayan Lepas airport. He was to fly from Penang to Singapore, to meet a friend Tauh who worked in a Bank in Singapore. He will then stay in Tauh house for a couple of days before flying to London, in a Union D'Transport Airline. Union D'Transport Airline is a French Airline.

The day finally arrived. Everything went as planned. It was afternoon around 4.00pm. Otard luggage was all packed and he was ready to go. Otard's father Rovivrus gave him a RM50.00 ang pow before he left for the journey. This is all Rovivrus could afford. Otard was from a poor family. They only have enough to eat, drink and wear, and of course a roof under their head. What ever Otard have was what he earned and saved.

Gnoy called at Otard's residence and the journey began. Otard put the luggage in the trunk of the car and Otard's father, step-mother and step-sister got into the back seat of the car, and Otard sat in the front seat next to Gnoy. They head for Bayan Lepas. They arrived there at the airport around 5.30pm. The MAS plane took off around 6.30pm, so there were ample time to say Good Bye. Otard mind was thinking, was it for better or worse. How would he find life in the far distant land called London. One thing Otard felt was freedom and he was free from the control of his step-mother Nae. He did not know whether to laugh his heart out, or to cry. It was an emotional moment.

The tense and troubled moments were short. Otard checked in his luggage, and boarded the plane. It was a small propeller aircraft, a Hawker Friendship. Otard is not used to travelling. He suffers from travelling sickness. He was sick when the plane took off and the flight called at almost every stop a in every state till it reach Singapore. He forgot about all his emotions and problems, only wishing the plane would land and got off the plane. To make matter worse, there was a thunder storm, and the plane wobble, heavily. The plane called at Singapore at around 9.00pm, and his friend Tauh was there waiting for him.

Tauh, took him to his house to bath and change before going out for supper. Tauh introduce him to his father a

Butcher. Tauh father was most friendly. He wore a blue short pants and a singlet. We did not talk much. All Tauh father said was "My son always bring home man friends, never a female. I had made a match for him. He is getting married in a year or two." Otard went to take his bath and changed. They then went out to supper and Tauh showed Otard how Singapore looked like at night. After seeing the town at night, they went home. As Tauh had to report for work the next few days, he arranged for his friend who works in the Singapore Airline as Chief Cabin Stewart to show Otard around Singapore. He had a wonderful time at Singapore.

The vacation time had come to an end, and Otard have to depart for England. Tauh took Otard to the airport and there he boarded a flight for England. Otard bid Tauh farewell. The flight was comfortable but Otard was sick and he was not used it. It was a wide bodied jet. There were ample space to sleep and he slept through the journey till they called at France. Otard changed plane when the plane called at France and he took the flight to London. The plane arrived at London Heathrow airport at 11.00am London time. In the chaos and confusion for Otard and he lost his luggage. Otard could still not get off the travelling sickness. Essor waited for him at the airport.

They took the bus to the to the tube station. There they catch the tube to East Ham. From east Ham they catch the bus to Popular Nurses Hostel in the East End of London by the Black Wall Tunnel. We were greeted by her friend Yramesor and Gnohc. Otard took a shower and changed. They then went out to lunch. It is as if the mind in related coincidence was playing on the radio the song "When will I see you again?" sung by the Three Degrees and Esor friends was talking of Esor's relationship. The Television was playing "You are my first my last my everything" sung by Barry White.

Chapter 4

Marriage

Esor planned to marry Otard in two weeks time. It is only possible to register for marriage after two weeks residing in the district. The two weeks came up and they Otard and Esor got registered. During the registration, Esor laughed at the registrar when asked "Do you take this man as your husband?" Otard, took no notice that something was absolutely wrong. How could she Esor be laughing in such a serious and solemn situation. Otard has no idea that Esor was a puppet and her puppet master Charles whiting was laughing away that he had caught a fish in his daughter and she is getting married. Caught a fish is a Chinese saying meaning getting hitched. Otard did not know about Charles Whiting till later in his life when he encounter him in his work environment. She was reprimanded by the registrar immediately. It was just a simple registration, at the Register of Marriage and they then had a meal at the local pub and drank some beer. Her friends said "why not divorce her and marry me". Otard took no notice of that and ignore the words of her friends.

After their lunch, they head back to the Nurses Hostel. Otard then took a bubble bath. After the bubble bath Otard went to sleep. They stayed at the Nursed Hotel temporarily till they can find accommodation. On awakening from his sleep, Otard could not find his wife Esor. Otard was angry and scared. He was in a Nurses hostel and all girls, and no boys around. Otard was angry as she Esor had not left a message, as to where she was going. Otard was a very emotional man. He just don't know what to do, and was plum worried. Esor came back about 7.00pm and told him she was out with her friends, Yramesor and Gnohc. They went to East Ham. Otard behave badly, and demanded to be taken to East Ham that evening. He wanted to see how it look like. Esor took Otard to East Ham, and she bought him a belt. The Chinese have a traditional believe that when you buy a belt for some one you will tie him down and restrain him from having further affairs with other women. Otard was satisfied like a child, and was most happy. They returned back to the Nurses Hostel.

Esor and Otard were highly sex and full of passion and romance. They make love through out the night. They would go out to market together holding each other hands. She was not a good cook and so they eat spaghetti fried Chinese style. They would cuddle each other when ever she returns from work. Otard was madly in love with her. The days of enjoyment were short, as soon he had to report for work.

Chapter 5

Work

Some days passed, Esor than took Otard to central London, at Russel Square to see his employer, Nairb at the Center Hotels Personnel Office. Nairb was not there and he was attended to by his personnel assistant, a Philippinena. She was very helpful. The particular job at Essex had been taken, and they have relocated him to London. He was allocated to work at Regent Center Hotel at Carburton Street.

Otard was to start work at the Tartino Coffee Shop, under the management care of Leahcim Uioigroeg. He was a Greek Cypriot. He did not work directly with him but with his assistant manager Onoitna a Portuguese. Otard was assigned a job of cleaning up the tables and washing up. Onoitna upon finding Otard was good in English, and he was allowed to serve as a waiter. A week or two later Otard then was send into the kitchen to work with the chef. The chef was a from Thailand and gained a lot of experience and skills that way. It was a simple menu, like Piza, Omelets, Spaghetti, Soups, Steaks, and burgers. They also have pork chops, chicken chops and lamb chops.

The customers would que to have their lunch and dinner at the Tartino coffee Shop. The patrons are normally office staffs and workers who worked near by. They would use Diners Club card or Luncheon vouchers. They would eat Pizza like Parlemo, Slalmi, Prosucito and Spaghetti like Bolonaise or Napolitan. Some would have fish and chips. Then others would have T bone steaks or Serlion steaks. Of course this is accompanied with French fries and a salad. It was simple plain fast foods. They would have tomato soup or minestrone soups as starters. It was always busy during lunch time, and Otard and Oniitna only took their lunch break at 3.30 pm. A number of months later Otard was assigned to work with Yram a supervisor at he the room service. She is a very beautiful, and kind Irish lady.

Otard fiend who accompanied him to Kuala Lumpur for the interview at the British High Commission was also was successful in getting the job. He arrived in United Kingdom some time later after Otard arrival. He was also assigned to work at the same hotel where Otard is working. He works in the morning shift with Ahcnoc. She was a plum woman of enormous build. She was from Spain. Otard was working the afternoon shift. When vacation time came, there we staff tours to America and he joined the tour but Otard turned it down as he has a wife to support. After the tour, Otard friend decide to pack up and head for home, Malaysia. He found the job was not to his liking. Otard friend resigned.

Nearly a year passed and Esor found an accommodation at her friend's house. She was Anveor. At her house there was a bedsitter available. Esor rent the bedsitter. A child was born to Esor. It was a girl. Esor father suggested hoping that the child could be named after him. Esor father, Otard father –in -law named her Aniroc. He wanted the child to be named Aniroc Wal, after his surname. Otard objected to the idea, so the child name is named by his father-in-law and Otard surname followed behind. The child is then named Aniroc Auq, after Otard surname. Suddenly Otard's mind became upset, as this is for the first time his thoughts told him, he do not wished to incarnate. Otard believe that the baby was his incarnation. It was himself reborn as Aniroc Auq. Otard was a Buddhist, and believe in incarnation in its teachings. Otard did not understand what had happened is that they are playing with his thoughts and there is no God. Esor parents came to visit us. Esor mother Hol wanted the Samsonite suit case, so Otard gave it to her. They stayed for a month then went back home. Otard and Esor took leave for a month. A week later, Otard and Esor flew back to Malaysia. Otard and Esor stayed at Esoer parents house. Esor parents threw a dinner and all relatives and friend were called. Otard parents was also threw a small dinner for the Esor family only, at Hotel Mandarin, Penang.

Some days later Otard returned home to his parents house. On impulse, Otard went upstairs to his bed room and opened the door. He then opened the door of the cupboard left by his mother to find a picture frame with a photograph of himself Otard and Eel were kept. He was deeply in love with Eel at one time. He quickly dismantled the picture frame and destroyed the photograph. He then took out the album with photographs of himself Otard and Eel and tore it up and destroyed it. Otard cried as he did this, but his mind was fixed on England, and the lifestyle there. Otard then drove past Notsgink house where Eel was residing. He was about to call on her when he saw Eel, hanging clothes and some nappies at the verandah. His thoughts told him that she had married the brother of Notsgnik and had born a child. Eel had married Mordo. It was rumored that Otard so loved Eel that his Astral Soul travelled down from London and enter Mordo body. In that event Mordo had sex with Eel and born a baby girl. The month of vacation came to an end and Otard and Esor had to return to England. Their daughter Anrioc Auq was left in the care of Esor mother. The child was classified British, as she used a British Passport. The child could not stay for long as she was a British Citizen. Otard had failed to register her at the Malaysian High commission.

On returned to England Otard together with Esor went to register the child, Aniroc Auq with the Malaysian High Commission. The child now have dual citizenship till she reached maturity to choose her citizenship. Otard boss, the Restaurant manager Leahcim sold him one of his used car, a blue Morris Minor. Otard was using International License to drive the car till he was stopped by the London Metropolitan Police and was finned British Sterling 60.00Pounds. He was told to get a British License which Otard finally did. The car broke down after six months. The car came to no value and so Otard sold it to the night bell hop assistant supervisor, Demahom who works night shift in the hotel where Otard's work., He was an Egyptain.

Two years passed by. Otard purchased a maisonette. The maisonette was located at Churston Avenue. It was located at the ground floor. It is a one bed room maisonette. Esor gave birth to another girl. Once a again Otard and Esor seek her father Otard father –in-law for a name for their daughter. This time he named her Anirbus Auq. Esor mother visited us again. This time Esor father did not visit us. She helped us care for the children. Esor has stopped working. Otard was now night coffee shop assistant manager. Otard works at night and sleeps in the day. The life style was bad. The maisonette also suffered rising dam during winter. Otard then went to study English Law A level, at Old Street College of higher Education in the evening before going to work. Otard was trying to get out of this night job. He later became the Night coffee shop

Manager and assistant Restaurant Manager to the Tapestry Grill. Though condition was bad, Otard stuck on the job for five years. He had to stick on for 5 years to gain UK residence. He got his permanent residence. He was working on a work permit and impossible to change job or hop around. Otard did not like the maisonette that much, so he sold it to a school teacher and buy a house at the East End. He purchased a house in Upton Park Road closed to the West Ham football stadium. The house is accessible at the Upton Park Tube Station. It is a two story house with an additional one story of attic room. Otard bought it with some furniture attached in the purchase. It has a front garden, and a back yard which is very big. He could see the train runs across the end of the back yard. The house has two rooms, and one attic guest room. It also has a basement store room. The house comes with a garage.

Otard wanted a better life than just working at night at the Tartino coffee Shop located at Regent Center Hotel. Otard found a vacancy at the local job center for an assistant catering manager at Ilford Palais, owned and managed by Mecca Leisure. Mecca leisure own a number of Entertainment outlets, not the mentioned the famous and well know Empire Ball Room. Of course, Otard applied for the position. The pay was no so good, but he wanted to get out of working Night at the Tartino Coffee Shop. He wanted to have more time with his family. Otard took up the job. He starts work at 3.00pm and ends work at 1.00—to 2.00am the following morning. Otard was quite happy with the job. He met a colleague in the work place, as head porter. He was Weis. He lived near to where Otard stayed. They get along very well. The manager there was Yrral. He was paralytic. He is a habitual drinker. Weis hates him. After six months Otard found that this is not the job he wants. The work hours was too long and the pay was not good. Otard desires to have more time with his family. Mecca Leisure sold its entertainment outlets to Thorn EMI Music Leisure and Dancing. With the change of Management Otard grasp the opportunity to work at Empire Ballroom, the largest Discotheque in Europe. He left Ilford Palais and joined Empire Ballroom.

There he started work at 8.00am and finished around 2.00am the following day. He got to receive the spirits delivery and the wine and beer delivery besides soft drinks in the early morning. They do not have a store keeper. The cellar man only looks after the draught beer delivery. The true pale ale Worthington E is a favorite to the patrons. He had his break at 4.00pm to 5.30pm. Normally all the staffs went to the local pub to pass their time, but the management are not to mingle with the staffs or to patronize the same pub. On joining Empire Ballroom after a couple of months, he was given the opportunity to run a wine bar, at the basement of the Ballroom. The Wine Bar was called Cast Away.

The business was not picking up compare to a wine bar some distance away from the Cast Away. Cork and Bottle Wine Bar was a competitor. At this time, Otard have no brain of his own, he was just a puppet, though he knows not who the Puppet Master nor does he know he is a puppet. They have some functions held at the Cast Away at year ends where Otard managed. They have the launching of Lamb's Navy Rum, Group Four Security annual Christmas Dinner and not the mentioned World Disco Dancing Championship press Conference and a few others. The World Disco Dancing championship was held at the Ball Room above the Castaway Wine Bar. Staffs were hard to find, they come and they go, all were part-timers. Otard hates losing some of the good par-timers.

Otard decides to resigned and look for a new job. Otard could not afford to be out of a job, and there are many financial obligations. Mortgage to pay, Electric bill to pay, gas bill to pay etc. Esor mother came by and visited us all the way from Malaysia once more time. She said the house is a bit dark and not good for the Feng Shui. Otard also bought a used car, from his colleague Weis, a Reanult TR30. It is in immaculate condition as inspected by Esor cousin Snake.

Otard found a job with Associated Fisheries. He was offered an Assistant manager position at the Seafarer Restaurant. They sell Fish and Chips delicacies. They have plaice and chips, rock eel and chips, haddock and chips, skate and chips and pickled onions. He was assigned to work at Romford. After some months he was transferred to work at Walthamstow then to the company Chelsea Outlet. Chelsea is the only shop in the chain that sells wine with the food.

Five years ago his life was all gloomy and unbearable. He had many unanswered questions. At 27 nothing exciting was happening to him. His career, finances and relationship left nothing to him to desire. He was stuck. His dream of struggling of travelling abroad and studying was to no avail. His job was boring and routine like. His finances was just hand to mouth. Then after many disappointments he was giving up. While working there Otard finds at the local job center that the Manpower Service Commission was offering training to upgrade Food and Beverages skill. Otard offered his resignation and applied for the training course. These is where the start of his problems begins.

Otard had the least idea what was in store for him. He was only a puppet. The time was not right. The puppet master wanted him in England and the meeting of his match. They have got a match for him. Now the time was perfect. They have located him and the girl whom was Otard tie since his birth.

Chapter 6

The Great Expectations

Otard, applied for the training. Otard wanted to improve himself. The training is a one year course conducted at Bolton Technical College, in Bolton, Lancashire. Otard was accepted for the training. He resigned from his job as Assistant Restaurant Manager at Seafarer Restaurant to attend the training. Otard did not know that his mind had planned for this course of action. Otard told Esor he was going to attend the training provided by the Manpower Service Commission.

Otard journey to Bolton a week earlier before the course to seek accommodation. He found a bedsitter at 6 Glade Street, in Bolton. Otard paid a deposit of one month rental in advance and one month rent for the accommodation. He then returned to his house in Upton Park, London. At the end of September falls, Otard left his family in London and went to attend the training course. He will become a professionally train skilled caterer Otard thought to himself. Otard arrived at 6 Glade Street one day earlier. He drove all the way to Bolton. Together with his luggage, Otard also brought with him a image statue of Buddha which he places on his writing desk at the bedsitter. The landlord referred to him as Buddha. Otard never knew that the residents of Bolton and the people who live within the area were sinister in their thoughts about Buddha and they desired him to incarnate. It was a plan to get him reborn. Otard never knew that. He was clean and innocent. The people of Bolton have other plans for him.

His college day begins at the end of September 1979. This was the first time he attended such training by the Manpower Service Commission. His class Tutor was Etihw. Etihw called out the names, and marked the attendance. Otard was sitting at the corner at the end of the class. There was a few man students, and the rest female students. The male students are, Kcaj, Snave, Divad and Otard himself. The female students were Ecyoj, Nerak, Eniluap, Delilah cold as ice, Ydnew, EiluJ and Eoj.

Some strange things start to happen. Otard head a voice said, she Dililah is the one, and he can also hear Dililah friends murmured he, Otard is the one. Otard took no notice of the event. To him it was just pure imagination. The course consists of City & Guild, 706 and 707 and National Examinations Board Supervisory Studies. With this courses, he will get membership in the Cookery and Food Association and Institute of Supervisory Management. To Otard this was his great expectations.

After the marking of attendance and briefing, they were showed around the facilities. Each one is allocated a locker to keep their tools use in the culinary and books. The then have a break. During the break they sat in the canteen to have their meals. After their meals, the mingled around the corridors. During that time Otard mind pick up thoughts as if he could not believe in his ears, Eoj, a friend of Delilah was knitting a shawl, and she was mumbling to herself, "I knit you Otard toward me Delilah Cold as ice." Of course, Otard took no notice of this event, and by passed it. Otard dare not approached Eoj to ask why she mumbled this words. Otard, let it be. The puppet master were at work. His thoughts told him Joe is a witch. Delilah cold as Ice is the daughter of darkness.

Eoj, carried on this chanting and mumbling daily. Delilah Cold as Ice, spent her evening or afternoon playing badminton with her friends Enilaup and Ydnew. This would carried on throughout the year, as if it was a ritual. It was first semester and Otard progress was good. He did well in all subjects except cooking. Otard can not get the idea of food presentation, and understanding the cookery jargon. Else all was good for Otard. The Second semester came, and Otard could not remove his gaze for Delilah, as she sat in a seductive position. She would like to sit with her legs wide apart, showing the forbidden parts of the anatomy. At this time, Kelali was the puppet master behind Otard's brain motivating Otard to like Delilah Cold as Ice. Otard brain Kelali likes Delilah Cold as Ice. Otard did not know about Kelali till his later days when they met, in another country. Otard was not furious, but became attracted to her. Term breaks came, and Otard drove home to London to see his wife and children.

Otard reached home and his wife Esor greeted him, and she wanted to go to bed immediately with Otard. Otard was not in the mood for love. All he wanted was his dinner. After dinner, they wash up the plates and utensils. Otard then took his bath then went to bed with Esor. They made love, and when Otard reach climax Otard could hear Delilah screamed, he wanted me, how dare he made love with another woman. Otard kept to himself and did not mentioned a single word to his wife Esor. A week passed, and Otard returned to Bolton.

Things start to get worse for Otard. His feelings grew for Delilah. Otard never felt an emotions like this before even when he was with Eel, or Esor. Otard was torn between Love and studies. Otard was shy, to confess his feelings for Delilah. Otard never felt like this before, even with his wife or the girlfriend Eel, he had before. It was totally a different kind of feelings. It is because of all these, Otard decide to write to Delilah to express his emotions and feelings. She never replied Otard correspondence or talk to Otard about the letters. Otard than gave her a photograph of himself. She took the picture and rejected Otard. Otard than requested her to return the photographs and letters, she refused.

Otard then as if he was possessed after college hours, he immediately after college drove to her house in Daisy Hill West Houghton. Otard had never been there before nor anyone told him of the address. She rejected him again. Twice after college hours, Otard drove to her house which was a far distant from his rented accommodation in another town, which Otard had never seen or visited before. Twice she rejected him. Then the college project came up. They have a weekend away from the college at a small town away from Bolton at Altrimham. When the study time is over, we played a game. The game came with a song, "The Grand Old Duke OF York". We sang the song and play the action, and those who failed were told to strip off one piece of their clothing. Delilah abstain from the game. We took a lot of photographs during the weekend.

It was back to college. The college seems not alright, as something does not seem right. Lots of students and teacher was getting pregnant. When ever Otard passed by, he could hear them scream Orgy, Orgy Orgy. Their aim is to born the old puppet master Het and remove hime from the present control of the world government system. Otard developed the photographs and put it in an album. With impulse Otard start to paste news paper clippings, flyers and brochures on to the album next to those photographs taken at Altrimham. Otard used to patronize the local Chinese Take Away. They also started to acted strange. Otard could hear their thought said he is In Love and still do not know how to make with Delilah so the price of fried rice have to increase. Otard find that all the people were against him, and none was with him or for him. They want to destroy the brain. During one class Session, Delilah complained to Alexis Saunders who then screamed at Otard over his behavior and his love affair for Delilah. Aexis Saunders was a Warlock and a Sorcerer. He was a very good friend of Eoj and together they get on very well.

One day on his way to college Otard purchased the local newspaper. He opened and read an article of Achilles. It read: "Achilles was the best fighter of the Greeks besieging Troy in the Trojan War. When the hero Odysseus journeyed to the underworld to seek advice of the dead prophet Teiresisas, he encountered the shades of Archilles. This hero had slain the Trojan God Hero Hector in a single combat and had himself been brought down only by the convenience of Apollo. The god guided the arrow of Hector's brother Paris to the only vulnerable spot on Achilles body – his heel." Immediately after reading the materials on the paper Otard felt his Achilles tendon crammed and sprained his ankle. Otard carried on as normal, and took no suspicion of the happening. He purchase a bottle of Sloane and rub on his ankle.

As this was the final semester, we had to sit for exams, practical and theory. In the stress, Otard did badly. Otard then saw in the Pharmacy they were selling Red Koga Ginseng, and he purchased a box to help him over come the situation. Otard still returned to his home where he had a wife and two daughters each weekend.

Normally, Otard would go to the laundry to do his laundry before driving home to London. On this particular night, at the launderette he saw a girl with an empty plastic container containing a vehicle overturned in the tub which she placed on the floor. Otard took no notice of the incident and carried on as normal, though his mind tells him this is his car. After the laundry Otard went home, and was ready to drive to London. He heard a voice telling him not to leave the parameters of Bolton. He took no notice of the voice. Otard returned home to the rented bedsitter at Glade Street after the laundry. Otard packed his bag and heads for his home in London where his wife Esor and children reside.

He came out of the rented bedsitter, and drove his car to London. As he was heading for London, he felt drowsy and his car went lopsided and nearly overturned. It was snowing. Otard drove on. As he reached the outskirts of Manchester, his car anti-freeze bottle edploded. Otard paid thanks to God he did not suffer any injury, but his car is gone. The radiator bottle exploded and the whole engine jammed. Otard lost his car and has no more transport.

They wanted make a new world order, and an old religion being brought to life and destroying them present brain. Otard was caught in between. Following this events on 27th august 1979 Lord Mountbatten was murdered. The Earl's twin grandson Nicholas 14 and an employee on the a boat Paul Maxwell 15 died in the incident. Lord Mountbatten was going lobster potting and tuna fishing in his 30 foot (9.1 m) wooden boat. The boat Shadow V was marooned at the harbor Mullaymore. Hours followed 18 soldiers well killed by a bomb blast at Warrenpoint border with the Irish Republic.

On 8th December 1980, John Lenon returning with his wife Yoko Ono from the Record Plant Studio was shot by David Chapman at the archway of the building the Dakota New York. Then President Ronald Regan of America was shot on 30th March 1981 by John Hickely while leaving a speaking engagement at Washington Hilton Hotel, Washington DC. This followed the Pope John Paul was shot and was wounded on 13th May 1981, in St Peter's Square by Mehmet Ali ass he was entering the Square. They were on the elimination lsit because they were children and puppets belonging to the puppet master oppose to Irani. Their puppet master were pro American and Isreal. Irnai was with the old religion. Otard still had no idea of the puppet master at work, nor does he know Irani, till his latter days.

Otard was a scapegoat and he did not know that he was referred to as God by the Boltianans. This was done long ago before he came to Bolton. He had been blame as a God, Buddha, Christ since childhood. The world is a stage and each of us must play a part and that was a part the people in Bolton and the world choose for him. They want the child to be born. He began to do badly in his college work and exams. He began to get interested in the occult and ancient mysteries. Ho bought lot of books on the subject and read through them and forgetting his studies. He also purchased a lot of kitchen utensils. One early morning, in his rented bedsitter around 5.00am, he heard drums being played out side his rented bedsitter. He woke up and opened the window an d he saw a lorry with some of the locals dawn in old traditional costumes beating the drums. It was as if they were performing a ritual or ceremony. He heard them said "he has opened the window and saw us, now we can move on". In Otard mind he could see a man being apprehended and taken to a Wickerman ceremony where he is burnt to death and Otard was supposed to be the one.

Otard never believe in witchcraft or Deadly Sorcery. Otard was all scared. Otard guess he was the most frightened man in the world at that time. Otard takes it that he had read too much on the subject of witchcraft, sorcery, black magic and mythology mysteries.

Daily, the students talked about the mind becoming pregnant, as they look at the news paper with the picture of a pregnant woman. Delilah would then converse with Eoj, about what they did at night, and how nice it was, and their boyfriend could not wake up the following day, even with ten cups of strong black coffee. Otard could not understand what they were talking about. They were trying to make Otard jealous and envious of their night sex life.

A hostage crisis developed in Iran. The Iran hostage crisis was a diplomatic crisis between Iran and the United States. More than sixty American diplomats and citizens were held hostage for 444days(November 4, 1979 to January 20,1981) after a group of Iranian students belonging to the Muslim Student followers of the Imam's Line, who supported the Iranian Revolution, took over the U.S. Embassy in Tehran. The was the work of the puppet master Irani.

The crisis was described by the Western Media as an "entanglement" of vengeance and mutual incomprehension. President Jimmy Carter called the hostages "victim of terrorism and anarchy" and said "The Unites States will not yield to blackmail". In Iran, it was widely seen as a blow against the United States and its influences in Iran, including it perceived attempts to undermine the Iranian Revolution and its longstanding support of the recently overthrown Shah of Iran, Mohamed Reza Pahlavi, who led and autocratic regime.

After the Shah was over thrown he was admitted in to the United States for cancer treatment. Iran dedanded that he be returned to stand trial for crimes he was accused of committing during his reign. Specially, Pahlavi was accused of committing crimes against Iranian citizens with the help of his secret police, the SAVAK. Iranians saw the decision to grant him asylum as American complicity in those atrocities. In the United States, the hostage-taking was seen as an egregious violation of the principles of International law, which granted diplomats immunity from arrest and made diplomatic compounds inviolable, after failed efforts to negotiate hostages' release, the United States military attempted a rescue operation using ships, including the USS Nimitz and USS Coral Sea, that were patrolling the waters near Iran. On April 24, 1980, the attempt, known as Operation Eagle Claw, failed, resulting the death of eight Americans servicemen and one Iranian civilian, as well as destruction of two aircraft. Documents dated two weeks before the operation claim that the American national security advisor Zbigniew Brzeinski, discussed an invasion of Iran through Turkish bases and territory, though this plan was not executed.

Shah Pahlavi left the United States in December 1979 and was ultimately granted asylum in Egypt, where he died of complications of cancer on July 27, 1980. In September 1980, the Iraqi military invaded Iran, beginning the Iran-Iraq war. The old and original puppet master that is pro American and Israel reacted and act against Iran with what they have after the fall of pro isreal American Iran. Algeria was chosen to act as mediator. The hostages were formally released into the United States custody the day after the signing of the Algiers Accords, just minutes after the new American president, Ronald Regan, was sworn into office. The shah Pahlavi was considered pro American Israel regime and was a children of the old puppet master who monopolies the American and Israel control oppose by Irani the New Puppet Master.

The crisis is considered a pivotal episode in the history of Iran –United States relations. Political analysts cite it as a major factor in the trajectory of Jimmy Carter's presidency and his lost in the 1980 presidential election. In Iran, the crisis strengthened the prestige of Ayatollah Ruhollah Khomeini and the political power of those who opposed any normalization of relations with the West. The crisis also led to the United States economic sanctions against Iran, further weakening the ties between the two countries. Ayatollah Ruhollah Khomeini is the father of the old religion and the favor of Irani the puppet master in all its manipulations and actions. Iranni puppet Ayatollah Ruhollah Khomeini now manipulates America.

Then came the Iranian Embassy Siege taking place from 30th April to 5 May 1980, after a group of six armed men stormed the Iranian embassy in South Kensington, London. The gunmen took 26 hostage- mostly embassy staff, but several visitors and a police officer who has been guarding the embassy, was also held. The hostage-takers, members of Iranian Arab Group campaigning for Arab national sovereignty in the southern region of Khuzestan Province, demanding the release of Arab prisoners from, jails in Khuzestan and their safe passage off the United Kingdom. The British Government quickly resolved that safe passage would not be granted, and a siege ensued. Over the following days, police negotiators secured the release of five hostages in exchange for minor concessions, such as broadcasting the hostage-takers demands on British Television.

BY the sixth day of the siege the gunmen had become increasingly frustrated at the lack of progress in meeting their demands. That evening, they killed one of the hostages and threw his body out of the embassy. As a result the British Govenrment ordered the Special Air Servvice (SAS), a special force regiment of the British Army to conduct an assault to rescue the remaining hostages. Shortly afterwards, soldiers abseiled from the roof of the building and forced entry through the windows. During the 17-minute raid, the SAS rescued all but one of the remaining hostages, and killed five of the six terrorists. The soldiers subsequently faced accusations that they unnecessary killed two of the terrorists, but an inquest into the deaths eventually cleared the SAS of any wrongdoing. The remaining terrorist was prosecuted and served 27 years in British Prisons.

The hostage-takers and their cause were largely forgotten after the Iran-Iraq War broke out later that year and the hostage crisis in Tehran continue until January 1981. Nonetheless, the operation brought the SAS to the public eye for the first time and bolstered the reputation of Margaret Thatcher, the Prime Minister. The SAS was quickly overwhelmed by the number of applications it received from people inspired by the operation and, at the same time, experienced greater demand for its expertise from foreign governments. The building, having suffered major damage from a fire that broke out during the assault, as a result the Iranian embassy close until 1993.

These was all the work of the puppet masters. Otard did not sense anything was wrong nor any connections to all these. To him it was just a world events taking place. These was the setting for the years to come for the change of a world order in a vast eternal plans, for a new Millennium by those who project the thoughts. Otard did not know he was refer to as God, and he is supposed to marry and make with the Devil woman Delilah and die after making love, like the king bee with the queen bee. Irani and its puppet master focused on Otard as the God of Israel and pro American and must be gotten rid off. Otard did not know that Irani drew his plans for world dominations. Otard did not know that Irani will be the super brain, the puppet master controlling the world situations. Otard did not know who he was, till he encountered his puppets Goaul Hati and Discota at a later part of his life. Even Goual Hati and Mrs Discota were his puppets. There job was to destroy Otard, or to get rid to him, to make way for a new millennium, and full fill the prophecy of their ancient teachings. It was as if the holy book tells us in Revelation, the end of Christ Kingdom and the birth of anti Christ. Irani hates Jews, so is of his puppets Kelali bin Mohamed Dawood. He also Otard encounters at a later days in his life. Delilah was the child of Irani. The whole of Boltn, all it residents were his puppets.

Chapter 7

The returned to London

College comes to an end, and Otard returns to London. The old puppet master Het looses heavily, and so Otard have to returned to the source of the orginal problem. Otard did badly in the exams, and his thoughts were troubled. Anyway he was admitted membership in the the Cookery and Food Association and Affiliate Membership into the Institute of Management. Otard thought he had left all the problems behind and the danger is over. He spent time with his wife Esor and daughters Aniroc and Anribas. He never disclosed to them all that happens in Bolton. His wife Esor wanted to take the children with her to returned to Malaysia. Otard was unhappy. He wanted to live in England. He do not want to returned to Malaysia just yet. He told his wife he is looking for a job, and everything will be alright.

He found a vacancy in Pool Dorset at the local hotel there. He catch a train to Pool, from Upton Park to Paddington then from there to Pool. He waited for an hour. There was no train. Then he saw a train parked near the platform and a front portion of the train were the engine was reversing backwards. He heard in his head that they are waiting for Lucifer. To Otard this was just a wild imagination. Finally, the train moves to the platform and take off carrying Otard and all the other people waiting. It was snowing. As the train moves, Otard feel his limbs become numb. By the time the train arrived at Pool, Dorset, was frozen stiff and could not move. He could not get off the rain. He call for the attention of the conductor who helped him off the train. He wanted to called an ambulance to take him to the nearest hospital. As it is a small town, and the ambulance was on call and none as available, so they call him a taxi.

The taxi driver was very good. He took him to the hospital and helped him of the taxi and got him a wheel chair and wheels him to the emergency reception. The nurse put him on a bed and pushed him to a cubicle where the doctor examined him. The doctor told him to rest there for some time. After an hour or two the doctor check on him again. He was now able to walk. He was discharged from the hospital. He phoned the hotel to tell them what happens and had his appointment postponed to a later time. The receptionist answered and transferred the call to the Human Resource Manager. She told Otard to attend the interview now if he is well enough to make it which Otard did. She offered the job to Otard at the interview and Otard said, he will consider as he had do discussed with his wife.

Otrad catch a train and returned home to London to his family. They then had dinner and after dinner his wife wanted to move the television to the second hall for the living room. Otard lifted the television and he felt weak and nearly dropped the television but finally got it to the second hall. Otard thought it must be the weather that has got the best of him, so he took some brandy and went to bed.

He woke up in the middle of the night and wanted to go to the wash room. He collapsed again. He told his wife to call their family doctor. The Dotor on called came an attend to him and asked if his parents is diabetic which he answer positive. The doctor said it is best for him to be admitted to the hospital in the morning. The doctor arranged for an ambulance to pick him up. His wife Esor was all shaken up and panic. As she was preparing breakfast in the morning, she cut her hand accidently. The Ambulance came and took Otard to hospital and his wife followed.

A lot of Otard friends all over the world fell sick as well. They were down with what sickness no body knows. Otard than found out one of his friend Ook, his father who had the same name as Otard'f father suffered from the same sickness as Otard, though he is in Penang, thousand of miles away from Otard. This is what you would say, when you fall in love, and your legs feel week. They said love can bring down a Giant to his knees. All those friends of Otard sick at the same time, were part and parcel of Otard old brain.

Otard and his wife Esor arrived at the hospital Saint Andrew located at Bromly by Bow and was admitted into the emergency ward. He was surrounded by a bunch of female doctors. His wife Esor went to have her cut treated. The female doctors examined him and do not know what is the course of the numbness. The doctors left and then lunch was served. He had lunch. Then came the doctors again after lunch this time with their Professor. The doctors was Dr Saunders, Dr Taran and Dr Fatimah. In Otard mind, his brain was telling him, he had a stroke or Polio. This made Otard worried. This made him wonder and ponder what he is going to do, for an Alien in overseas away from home. The Professor was Charles Persoff. The Professor asked the young and beautiful doctors "What was wrong with the patient?", none of them could give a correct answer, though the doctors described their diagnosis. Immediately the Professor Charles Perssoff told the doctors that it was an over active thyroid problems. He described the symptoms and the swelling of the neck indicate the cause of the numbness. This brought a relief to Otard mind, and he was most happy when he heard what the Professor told the doctors. He now know he don't suffer from polio or stroke.

He then prescribed medications for treatment. He then mentioned that if this does not cure the next course of action would be is operate. The first medications given to him cause allergy. It did not work, he collapsed again that night when he tried to get out of bed and got to the wash room. Then, he was prescribed Propythyrocil. This worked on him and he recovered quickly. He loved his wife dearly and missed them and he was allowed to go home every weekend for the afternoon during his treatment at the hospital. He was there for three weeks before he was discharged.

Otard was jobless for a month. And he decided to take a vacation to Germany to visit his sister friend Llib. When he arrived at at Germany Koblenz he caught at tramp to the Max Planck Institute to visit Llib. Llib was no there when he arrived at the Max Planck Institute. He was out with his friend to buy a Love Bug, the Volx Wagon beetle. The house master at the Max Planck institute attended to him and showed him to the guest house. He stayed there for a couple of days then flew back to London. While in Germany, Llib, took him to see the town and showed him around. They have sausage for lunch and dinner at the institute. To Otard this was not enough for his stomach so he went down town to have a roast chicken to fill his stomach. Llib was working at Max Planck Institute. He is a Microbiologist. Soon Otard vacation was over and so he flew back to London. The flight was horrible for Otard, as he suffers from Travel Sickness.

Esaor was firm in leaving for Malaysia. Otard applied for a job at Flemings Hotel, as Assistant Manager. He was interview by Lawrence Dunn, and he was accepted. Mr Dunn was the food and Beverage Manager. The General

Manager is Harish Paurana. Before him was his brother Jay, who left to work in some Kenya Mine. Harish was not well versed in the hotel, he come from the Ford factory where he worked before as Otard was told. The Managing Director is Goaul Hati. His secretary is Mandy Hew. The receptionist are, Susan Lavender, sue Mitchell, Karen Farr, Karen Parkinson, Sylvia and Evette. The Head housekeeper is Marget and her assistant is Mandy Amanda. Lawrence warned Otard to stay well clear of Harish Paurana and the linen woman Discota who works at the basement down below. And of course, the Accountant a Mr Singh and his assistant a Mr Patel.

Chapter 8

Work at Flemings Hotel

Otard reports for work at Flemings Hotel. There were two shift. The morning and the afternoon. Otard first day was in the afternoon shift. Otard do not understand the world is a stage and each of us must play a part. It is all in a game. The game of Death. Otard is not an actor or a star. All he wanted was to make a living and support his family. To him it was a job. He had no idea that the problems he had at Bolton with Delilah at the Bolton Technical College was not over. He had the least idea that Goaul Hati was playing God and his linen lady Mrs Discota who works in the basement was playing Devil. The brain of Goaul Hati is cursed by the name of Mad Ying. Otard does not know where Mad Ying came from till very late of his life, and brought him disaster. Whenever Goaul Hati moves we can hear him said, madness, madness complete madness blaring in his head.

Otard was caught right in between the God Goaul Hati and Devil Discota. He was like a puppet on a string. They the Thoughts Projectionist, Witches, Sorcerers, Magicians, Warlocks were the Puppets Master manipulates the situations. The Accountant Mr Singh would visit Otard in the Restaurant "The American Inn" every morning and questioned Otard "Was there any problems Mr Otard?" Otard would then reply," there was absolutely no problem".

Mr Singh would then order a cup of coffee where he would drink before carrying out his work. Delilah the daughter of darkness would be the Devil Discota and Goaul Hati would played God, and they both represent Otard. It is a game they all played, and Otard was the pawn.

After working for a week, Otard knee starts to gives him aches and pain. Otard did not know they wore him as Presphone as in the Greek mythology. Discota who played the Devil, also suffered similar aches and pains. It is all in a game, and Otard does not understand what the public desire. To Otard it was a job as assistant Food and Beverage Manager, that is assistant to Lawrence Dunn. He did not know they wanted him to produce a baby. It was a very complicated order. It was a mind game, they played on Otard.

They focused on Otard being Persephone. Presephone was the daughter of the Greek Mythology father Zeus. Her mother was Demeter. It is told in the Greek Mythology, Presephone forlicked with her friends upon the hillside, as her mother Demeter sat near by. Presphone thought to bring to her mother what they gathered, a handfuls of purple crocuses, royal blue and sweet smelling hyacinths. It is then said that Presophone was distracted by a vision of the most enchanting flower she had ever seen. It was narcissus, the exact flower hoped she would find. As she reached down to pluck it from its resting place, her feet began to tremble and the earth was split into two. Presphone life would never be the same again.

From this gaping cervice in the ground emerged the awe-inspiring God of the Underworld, Hades, and before Presphone could even think to utter a word, she was whisked off her feet onto the God's golden chariot. As he crack of the whip upon his majestic horses brought her to her senses, she realized she was about to be taken into the black depths from which he'd come. The thought of this brought terror to her heart, yet any screams and protest were soon lost in the darkness as they descended quickly unto the underworld below. This was the rape of Presephone, that brought the pains to the knee of Otard and Discota. It was a picture of her knee being grappled by the god of the underworld which the thought projectionist, warlocks and witches held holding Otards knee cap. None of this was spoken to Otard, it was all in the mind, and in the game, the people played.

Lawrence showed Otard how to carried out the work. After a few weeks working, Harish Paurana changed the work schedule to three days day work and four days rest and vice versa of four days work and three days rest alternately. Harish Paurana then discussed with Otard of seting up a screen portioning the coffee shop from the restaurant, by separation. He intended to purchase a Bamboo screen with reinforced with a leg of iron.

Some days followed, the wedding of Charless, Prince of Wales and Lady Diana Spenser took place on 29 July 1981 at St Paul's cathedral, London, England. The ceremony was a traditional Church of England wedding service. Notable figures in attendance included many members of royal families from across the world, republican heads of state, and members of bride and groom's families. Their marriage was widely billed as a "fairytale wedding" and the "wedding of the century". It was watched by an estimated global TV audience of 750 millions. The United Kingdom had a national holiday on that day to mark the wedding.

Otard did not notice or understand something's was absolutely wrong. They even approached Otard at the Flemings hotel, where he worked, when in the restaurant, whether he watched Prince Charles Wedding. On returning home,Otard starts to destroy the things he had in his house by burning them. The problems he had encounter at Bolton Technical college had returned. Otard bought a silver paint and painted on the mirror the Indian syllable OM. The mirror was part and parcel of the property when purchase off the previous owner. Esor wanted to rent the house out and returned to Malaysia, Penang. Esor found a tenant, and Indian from the Indian Government officials residing in England. Otard rejected the offered. Otard wanted to live in the property. Otard did not see what was in store for him, nor did he know what was planned for him.

Otard met a room guest in the hotel. His name was Charles Whiting. They exchange conversation, and he told Otard he was an International Lawyer and was here to mend the broken heart of a love of a girl, he represent. Charles Whiting invited Otard to dine with him for dinner, at the hotel restaurant that evening. Otard went into the dinning room to wait for him. On his way there, Otard could hear the voice of his father Rovivrus, telling hime to avoid that man Charles whiting. Charles Whiting came along when Otard was maneuvering to avoid him. He wanted to meet the chef at the Flemings Hotel, to cooked him a special meal. The following day, they had dinner a gain, Charles Whiting and Otard. The Chef Philip Tran cooked the dish of Vietnamese Prawns for him. Opposite the table sat a plum looking guest named Arnold Flow. Charles whiting told in Otard brain that Arnold Flow was the Goat of Mandes and ancient God whorhiped by the Satanist. It then came to Otard mind that Charles Whiting was the red god of Bahomet. Charles whiting told Otard to stir well clear of Arnold Flow and have nothing to do with him. Charles Whiting had a dislike for Arnold Flow. At the end of the dinner Chareles Whiting invited Otard to his room to watch television. Otard turned him down, and he returned to his room and Otard turned in for the night.

Esor was leaving with the two children, for Malaysia in a week's time. Otard felt depressed. Otard on impulse than starts to buy drawing paper and started to draw all kinds of drawings The following day Otard then out of no reason journey to Totenham Court Road to buy Marvel Comics. He bought all these comics at Forbiden Planet. In addition he for no reason walks down the road to Atlantic Book Shop and purchase books on the Occult. He also purchased some tracing paper. He never been there before.

One of the book he purchased was Secret Teachings of All Ages and the other was Holy Kabalah. He then went to Harrods and purchase a Tarot Deck on Seccret Teachings of the golden Dawn. He do not understand why he purchased all these, or how he knows where to get them. He then traced all these drawings and transferred on the cartridge drawing paper. It was as if he was possessed. It seems the picture he draw and traced out from the books came to life in the guests of the hotel where Otard works in. These carried on for days. It seems the people were made of paper. All kinds of events start to occurred in the hotel and strange thing start to take place in the world.

Otard wife Esor departs with the children, and she left a pair of sandals at the door. Esor told Otard as she was leaving, she had left her sandals at the door, and if he had no desire for them, he can throw it away. These was Otard heartache number one. The hall in Otard house came to be magnetized and every thing became magnetic. Otard did not understand it was mind over matter, and matter over mind. Otard did not understand his brain had fallen on the cartridge paper, and he is possessed, and being used by Charles Whiting and Arnold flow. Even though Charlees

Whiting and Arnold Flow were no on good terms with each other. They battle each other in the mind for supremacy. What Charles Whiting and Arnold Flow do not know nor understand that there is a bigger puppet master behind them and they are only puppets.

Otard was confused and angry. Why Esor was leaving, Otard could never understand. After Esor departs for Malaysia, Otard went to work as usual, at the Flemings Hotel. This time the Guest at the hotel known as Arnold Flow with his wife talked to Otard. He discussed with Otard about Charles Whiting then he told Otard to kiss the Jade ring which Otard wore on his finger. Arnold mentioned this a a pact between him Arnold Flow and Otard.

A few days passed and the hotel introduce an in house television channel. Otard was showed how to tune them and he had to tuned all the television in the Hotel. Otard did just that. For the past few days, the Assistant House Keeper Mandy Amanda wanted a room to stayed over night as she had forgot the keys to her house. Otard gave her a room and let her stayed overnight. These happened for a few evenings. Then Mandy Hew, the secretary of the Mr Gooul Hati secretary wanted a room to stayed overnight as well. Otard gave her a room. Otard styed overnight as well and he worked the four days shift. The Receptionist Susan Lavender and Karen Farr also stayed overnight. They stayed at room 405 and Otard stayed at room 306. At 2.00 am the fire alarm went off. Everybody leaves their room an assembled at the lobby. It turned to be a false alarm and so everyone returned back to their rooms. These also happens very often.

The waiter, barman and chef refused to turn up for work. Otard could hear in his head that they complained that they had so sex at night so no manpower. They all wanted Otard to chant intercourse for them, Philip Tran also has left and a new chef Debbie Waffle took over. Otardd had to cooked, serve and do some butchering. He master all this kills in the training he had at the Manpower Service Training, at Bolton. He remembered all that Margret White and Margret Steel had thought him at the college.

Lawrence Dunn the Assistant Manager resigned. He said he had enough with the hotel. Otard ccould hear them cutting his soul, by cutting him with their butchering knife, and the thought were real, as the knives could touch Otard body. Otard was at lost and knows not what action to take. He was fear of dying. Following all these happenings it was reported in the news that 8 Argentina's have landed on falklands. In 1982, Argentia which was ruled by military junta was facing an economic crisis. General Leopoldo Galtieri hoped an invasion would bolster his fading popularity at home. Tension first started to simmer when a group of Argentine scrap metal workers landed on British-controlled South Georgia 810 miles east of the Falklands, on March 19, and hoisted Argentina's blue-and-white national flag. Then, on 2 April, around 3,000 Argentine special forces invaded Port Stanley, the island capital. This invasion set the scene for conflict.

Otard still did not understand the situation that he was God and had to carry the armory of war for the Bristish. He never knew that, when he was in the tube, till one of the passenger said "He had a load to carry, better he sit down" and they gave up the seat for him. When he reached home, after work, he found his shoulder were bruised. Otard was a scapegoat, and was called a God not of his own choosing or desired. Otard carry on living as normal and took no notice of the situation he was in. He was to engrossed with his work and his family commitment. He wanted to have to feed his wife and children and a home to maintain.

A day later Otard had lunch at the hotel and his thoughts told him to munch in the food he was taking was the organs of Arnold Flow. After three mouthful Arnold Flow hit back and munched Otard organs. It was most painful. Otard don't feel well so he went to his room 306 to sleep it off. Otard woke up that evenings and found his physical form very light and as if he were transparent. He went down to the dinning room to have a soup, was all he could have as he was not well. At this time, in Malaysia, Otard's father was very ill and vomited through the evening. Otard found that his body was just a light. Hasrish Paurana told Otard to Evict a patron at the Bar, an English Lady named Elizabeth. Otard went to the bar to see her and inform her she is to leave the bar. She invited Otard to her accommodation at the the Navy club opposite. Otard turned down the offered.

The following day a new manager Thomas Mac greedy took over the place of Lawrence Dunn. Otard could not believe his eyes he had a tail and it look like white snake. Otard do not know how to get out of the situation or resigned. He was cooking breakfast that day. The chef did not report up for work. Otard felt being taken advantaged and had a bad time.

After cooking breakfast, Otard went to his office to get changed. His superior Harish Paurana called him into his office. He gave Otard the sacked and said he is mad. Otard took his things and left Flemings Hotel, at Half Moon Street. As he was leaving the front exit from the Hotel, He could hear the Managing director Goaul Hati saying to himself, "I am now Otard and your are no more Otard. Otard in now my name". It seems Goaul Hati wanted to be God. The brain of Otardd lost the battle and Otard did not know that the kingdom of Christ had fallen, and have to travel east to meet his final encounter but Otard have no idea what was planned for him. He is in the lost as to where he should go or what he should do.

Otard took the Tube home, and when he reached home, he found the security alarm blaring and he was scared just in case some one breaks into the house. He found an intruder in the house, who turned out to be a friend of his wife Esor. He was Iooh. He explained Otard wife gave him the keys to the house.

Chapter 9

The Return to Malaysia

Iooh, then asked Otard, "Are you still not going home to Malaysia?" Otard did not reply. Iooh, then went upstairs to the room belonging to the children of Otard Aniroc and Anirbas and changed and took his rest. He brought with him some pieces of Cassette he brought from Malaysia. The cassette contained the Songs from Alley Cats, and Iooh was playing it again and again, in the house. It was 7.00pm and Iooh came down stairs, and it sounded like he was talking to Esor mother Hol. Otard could hear him said, "He is still not dead and is sitting in the hall". Otard then pick Iooh thoughts, that Esor mother claims that Otard is dead in the center of the hall.

Iooh, then sing the malay song fluently from the cassette of Alley Cats for some time, then mention He and Otard would go to the Chinese Take Awway for dinner. Before Otard left for the Take Away, he opend the door of the fridge and foud the egg in the fridge had been tampered with. It seems the eggs had been prick with a needle. The thoughts of Otard was that the eggs had been poison. Otard was fearful for his life. He immediately obeyed the instruction of Iooh and followed what he wishes. They went to the Chinese Take Away. Iooh order mixed rice, and Otard followed. The mixed rice was cooked and was put into plastic container. They collected the rice and Otard paid for the meal.

They returned home to the house Otard Purchased, at Upton Park. Iooh played the cassette again as they eat the Chinese Take Away. The music and songs were hypnotic and had Otard bedazzled. Otard fearful for his life agreed to go home to Malaysia. Otard immediately requested Iooh assistance to purchase an air ticket to Malaysia. Iooh was most happy Otard seek his assistance to get and air ticket. Otard had lost all confidence to himself. It the first time, Otard was frightened of everything. The old brain of Otard the puppet master Het had lost heavily and have to retreat to his home land. Otard then took all the books down from the shelves including the set of Encyclopedia Britannica and took it to the kitchen back door near the garden. Otard had no idea of what he was doing, it was as if he was possessed.

During this process, Iooh, requested for the Sinclair Computer and the Vatman Boss Calculator that Otard purchased in the earlier days when he first came to London just after the born of thee first child. Immediately Otard giv in to his demands. Otard opens the back door, and took the books in the kitchen back door to the garden and set it ablaze. Otard was no more in control of himself. Everything in the house was brought down to the garden to burn. Otard brain has been taken over by some mysterious force.

The following day Iooh returned that evening with the Air Ticket. With the money Otard gave Iooh, he purchased an Air Pakistan ticket. They decide to have a dinner together before Otard finally depart for Malaysia. They went to an Indian Restaurant to have dinner. Otard continue with the burning as if his brain was under a spell. His brain was under psychic attack and he was hallucinating. All kinds of imagination creeps into his mind. He start to imagine people disappearing. Iooh was in command and control of the whole situation. After dinner, it was around 9.30 pm, they Iooh and Otard took a stroll down the neighborhood. At this time there was a war in Falklands and a race riot in London. In the thoughts Otard picked up was that the thoughts projectionist intend to destroy England with internal and external chaos.

The third days arrived, and Otard continue to burn his property. Iooh went out as usual. Otard did not eat at all. Iooh returns and played the Alley Cat cassette before they went out to the Chinese Take Aay and purchase some food to eat. They returned and have their dinner. After the dinner Iooh took the 4 inch vegetable knife up to his room and closed the door. Otard felt frightened. He could read the thoughts of Iooh pierce himself round his body with the knife. Otard went to sleep.

Otard wakes up late the next day, and Iooh was already out. Otard continue with the burning of his property. There was plenty of things to burn. Iooh came back,and inform Otard he is moving out the next morning. Otard lost his confidence, and was scared to be alone, though he did not informed Iooh. The burning continues. It was one more day before Otard depart for Malaysia. He burnt his GEC record player and all the records in his collection, his Hitachi cassette player and all his cassette collection. He also burnt his Alpha Amplifier and his Tec Tuner.

The next day came and Iooh left. Otard was all alone. Otard lost his wallet. He lost his mind and do not know what to do next. He tried to cook some vermicelli. He put the vermicelli in a sauce pan and turned on the gas. The fire lit. Otard was shocked in his eyes he could see his step sister Acirtap squat down over the drain and answer nature calls, in the old fashion bathroom in his parent's house. Otard saw her fecal oral matter dropped into the sauce pan where Otard was cooking his vermicelli. The water in the sauce pan turned brown. Otard lost his appetite and immediately threw everything away. He was frightened and angry. Otard did not have his lunch that day. He packed his bag and got his documents ready. The next day Otard will be leaving for Malaysia.

As Otard lost his wallet and he had no money so he went over next door to his Jamaican neighbor to borrow five pounds. His neighbor daughter Lorac loan him the five pounds. He went out to have a glass of milkshake. After the milkshake, he came home and found his wallet under the cushion, on the settee in the hall. He immediately took the five pounds and returned it to his neighbor's daughter Lorac. He, Otard continue to burn the furniture, and he even received thoughts to request him to commit suicide, by burning himself in the flames just like the way the priest did it during the Vietnam war.

Otard came to his senses, and realized his world has ended and not the world had ended. The local police called at Otard house that evening to extinguish the flames. Otard put out the fire and went to sleep. Otard brain representing the world brain whom they called God, and they have succeeded to destroy the brain without killing Otard, and so the brain can start afresh as a new brain represent the religion of the Old Gods. It is all set for the millennium a new brain they wanted so Otard had a new master. When he woke up the next morning, the whole house smell like gas. He quickly rush down to the kitchen to see the stove, and turn off the gas. He never touched the stove and never knew how the gas was turned on. Their mind have control over matter.

Otard took his bath and changed and get ready to go to Heathrow Airport. He got his air tickets and his luggage, he left the house in Upton Park and heads toward the tube Station. At the entrance to the station he met Esor friend Ycart and her husband Laniaz. Otard request them for assistance. Otard requested if they could help Otard get to the air port. They immediately turned down Otard request. Otard then went to purchase the tube ticket and on completion Otard head for the train. He went down a flight of stairs. He heard a voice said, the thing is coming.

On looking back, he saw a gas like bubble with bad words coming out of the bubble. The puff of gas over took Otard as he tried to enter the train, on the platform. The thing then began to scold Otard, with words like "You still not know how to sex me". The gas bubble touch Otard mouth. Otard was wondering if the other passenger saw what he sees, and witnessed what happened. It was a District Line train. Otard had to change train for Heathrow Airport at Leicester square. They were still playing with the brain of Otard. Otard was able to change train, and finally get to Heathrow Airport.

Chapter 10

The Flight

He checked in at Heathrow airport, and waited for the plane. Finally they were allowed to board the plane. The plane took off from Heathrow Airport and flew for some time in the air then landed to pick up more passengers. Otard was in hallucination. They pick up a group of passengers and one of them have features of the great Ayatollah Ruhollah Khomeini of Teheran. He sat next to Otard and their thoughts communicate with Otard.

During the flight, the man with the features of the great Ayatollah send thoughts to Otard to take off his shoe and slide it to him. In return he did the same. The man with the feature of Ayatollah began to wear Otard shoe and Otard with no choice, wore his shoe. Otard never understand what the was the actual purpose of the transaction. Its an English saying that you must be in his shoes to understand his problems, and thoughts. This took place for 25 minutes, and then he requested Otard to return his shoe which Otard did. He only returned one shoe of Otard and kept wearing the other shoe of Otard. Otard was furious and scare and know not what to do. About twenty minutes time Otard god his shoe back. The man with the feature of Ayatollah returned Otard shoe.

The flight landed a number of times. At one stop, all of the passengers came out of the plane and rested and the terminal. The boarding time came again. This time Otard thoughts questioned him, whoich plane he is boarding, Israel or Air Pakistan for Malaysia. Otard did not understand it was a changing of the brain for a new world order for the Millennium. Of course Otard chose Air Pakistan, as that what his air ticket was for Malaysia and he is a Malaysian.

Once that was settled, the plane took off. A few more stop over then he reached Subang International Airport at Kuala Lumpur. He have reached Malaysia. It was past midnight, in the early morning. Otard had missed his connecting flight for Penang. He spent the night at the airport. His thoughts told him while waiting for morning for the flight to Pulau Pinang, to watch a Silat Demonstration. He saw nothing. Then he walked toward the entrance of the airport facing the road. He saw the features of a man looks like Esor father Barry and a woman look like Esor mother Hol. They were waiting at the air port to pick up some friends. Otar nearly went to them thinking it was his father-in-law and mother-in-law but his sanity told him not to.

Soon itr was morning, Otard purchased an air ticket to Penang. He board the plane and flew to Penang. On arriving to Penang, Otard took a Taxi to his wife Esor residence. Otard surrender all his belonging to Esor father Barry. Esor mother made a cup of Milo for Otard and she offered him some Jacobs "Creeam Crackers. Esor was working at the Medical Center as a nurse said her mother. Esor mother Hol, told Otard to take a bath and rest upstairs. His wife will be coming home later.

Chapter 11

Malaysia

She told him his children had gone to school. They were styding at convent, a school near by the house. Otard went upstairs to take his bath and rest. Otard felt his body in flames, feel with burning love for his wife. Otard sleep till 3 pm then his wife returned and woke him up. She went to take her bath and have her lunch, then Otard and her went to bed and make love. After he make love, the feelings of burning love for his wife is gone. He felt nothing.….. everything was blank in his head. He never disclosed to his wife the events that succumbed his life while in UK.

That evening, Esor parents dropped Otard and Esor at Otard parents house. They were having a celebration of some kind. Otard, asked what the occasion was for, he was told, it is somebody's birthday. They eat till about 9.00pm then Otard and Esor parents came to pick them up to returned to Esor house. In Otard thoughts they are celebrating the birth of the new brain after the burning and destruction of the old brain in London.

Some days later Esor Aunt, sister of Esor's father took Otard and Esor to a movie. It was a Chinese Documentary. She explained to Otard in his thoughts that all these was his fault as he did not visualize Esor Cousin the Pyton as all these character in the Documentary. These is what had happened.

It was a battle of the thoughts between the English and the Chinese for supremacy. Now Otard understand what he was trying to learn, when he joined some organization and their teaching. They believe thoughts have wings. Otard now know he had missed out in all his studies and searching for cosmic knowledge. It was so simple.

He then realized he had to pull the cart and family to support. As he do not have any Malaysian qualification, it was most difficult for him to find a job with a good salary. There was no job available and he was most frightened and under stress. The old puppet master Het lost heavily, and his puppet Otard has no lively hood. Finally he found a job at E & O Hotel, as a supervisor at the restaurant, and the pay was very low, around RM600.00 per month. This is not even enough to feed himself not to mention his family. Otard was worried sick. There is rental to pay, electric bill to pay and water bill to pay, not to mention the daily groceries and food expenses for the family.

Otard returned home to his family house a coupled of times. Each time he returned home, he brought back his coins collections and stamps collections and gave it to his father-in-law. Esor father is a collector of coins and stamps. He is a collector of Antiques and souvenirs. His house looks like a museum or an antique shop.

Chapter 12

Bandar Sri Bagawan

Even with the job at E & O Hotel Otard was still job hunting. He saw an advertisement for a vacant position at Bandar Sri Bagawan. The Victor of the new Millennium was calling for him. The Irani brain, the new puppet master was searching and looking for Otard. He went for the interview. There was a few people there looking for similar positions. Otard applied for the position of Room Service Supervisor. He was then called for interview. After the interview, he walked home to his parents house where his father stayed with his second wife, Otard step mother.

On his way home to his parents house, Otard heard a voice calling him, "Do you want the job?". All you have to do is make love with the Interviewer, who is a woman. Her name was Haniaz. Otard agreed, and he could see some figure move into the room of Haniaz and make love. A few minutes later the phone ring at Otard parents residence informing him he got the job at Sheraton Utama Hotel at Bandar Sri Bagawan. The pay was only $850.00 Bandarr Sri Bagawan Dollar per month Bandar Sri Bagawan currency. There was no jobs in Malaysia, Penang, for Otard and he had to seek refuge in the land of the source of the old religion.

Otard did not have a choice, but to accept the job, as he is under pressure to have pocket money. An air ticket was forward to Otard and he flew to Bandar Sri Bagawan. A van was sent to pick him up at the airport and took him to the dormitory called white house. He was given a bed in the dormitory to share with some four people. Otard was not used to that and find it most in uncomfortable. The van pick them up the next morning and Otard report to the personnel office. He was given a set of uniform and introduce to the Catering Director a Mr Mel Macadle. He took Otard to the Room Service Office after Otard changed to his uniform. Otard was to be an Assistant Supervisor working with Derek Nimo.

Derek Nimo was away on leave and Otard was all alone, to work with the room stewards and a mini bar steward. The mini bar Stewart was Idris Ismail and the Room Stewarts was Kilali bin Mohamed Dawood, Abdul whaid, Sapari Labaja and Tony Anbutang Palatui, Jimmy Lim Ee Aun and Andrew Leong Yau Long. Jimmy Lim and Andrew Leong will be leaving for Malaysia in a months time, as their contract has ended. Otards found it was alright working with them on the first month.

In the dormitory, he met a boy from Malaysia Liew Tuck Foo. They befriended each other. He cooked Magi Mee that evening and they share the meal tighter for dinner. After eating Liew Ttuck Foo falls sleep. Otard received a letter from his wife, telling him not to come home to her parents house or her house as he is no longer welcome. Otard was scared now he has no wife and no friends and in a strange land. Otard could never understand why his wife wanted him no more. Otard felt sad. Jimmy Lim and Andrew Leong, introduced to Otard a waitress working at the Heritage Restaurant just opposite the Room Service

Office. She was Alice, and they became the best of friends as Otard was all alone, with no friend. In Otard brain it said she was provided to serve the Gods. Their friendship developed. Each evening after finishing work, they would go out to dinner together, and of the then to the movies.

One day in Room Service, Otard received a call to serve the room guest a plate of fried Singapore Mee Hoon. Otard places the order in the kitchen. When the order was ready, Otard took the plate and put it on the tray he prepared for the customer. Otard, took the tray of food to the customer bed room. He was surprised to see the man resembling the great Ayatollah Ruhollah Khomeini whom he encountered in the airplane on his trip returning to Malaysia. This man then starts to complain why he is served fried mee hoon which contains pork. The old man religion forbids him from eating pork. Otard explains he did not know he does not eat pork, and he did not mention that he abstain from pork when he places the order. He then stressed that the item in the menu should specify the food contains the presence of pork. Otard apologizes for the error in the menu and took the food back to the kitchen and convey the words of that man to the chefs. After the incident, he saw no more of that man. Otard finished work at 3pm and so he visited Alice room at the servants quarters. They went out to dinner then to the movie.

One of the movie Otard watched with Alice was Hell has no boundary. The story is about a man who battle his twin soul, who looks like him, and out to destroy him. It is a ghost story. When the movie finished, Alice and Otard walk back to their servant quarters. Alice contract expires, and so she left Bandar Sri Bagawan for home. Otard was all alone again. This was heart ache number two. Few months past and the Room Stewarts the staffs of Otard began to act strange. They refuse to cooperate with Otard or took orders from Otard. Otard can pick up their thoughts, saying they are waiting for the Otard to come inside them to work. To them this is not the one who loose. To them this is not that Otard from Uk, and they are looking forward for that Otard. One day they sat in the canteen and would not report for work and Otard went to see them and try to compromise with them. During the negotiations, the Catering Director Mel Macadle budge in and of course Otard got the blame for not being in the Room Service Office, and no one was at the post. This got Otard into trouble with the company and with Mel Macadle.

Otard wrote to Mel Macadle his resignation. The mini bar Stewart Idris sat in the room service office and told me his package he ordered will be due from Kuala Lumpur. What his thoughts is saying is he wanted a Girl friend from Malaysia, and she is the parcel coming on the way. One morning one of the room Stewart came and knock on the door of Otard Servant quarters, informing him that the catering director Mel Macadle wanted to see him.

He took his bath, got dressed and went to see Mel Macadle. He was informed he can leave now for Malaysia, and an air ticket has been purchased. He took the Air Ticket and left Mel Macadle Office, then he proceed to the Roomd Service to see who was his replacement. He found a girl there name Adeline Lim was the new room Service Supervisor. Otard went to pack his belongings and head for the van waiting for him. The van took him to airport. His former Malay staffs at the Room Service said they will be with him in thoughts. Otard thought that was good, and they are his friends. Otard does not know it was against the wishes of the Chinese people his parents and friends.

Otard

It was meant for Otard to settle down in Bandar Sri
Bagawan and start a home there. The Old puppet master got
back his form and recuperated and rescue Otard from the
land of the Old Religion. Otard was now free of his marital
commitments and free of the sex problems he experienced.

Chapter 13

In His Parent House

He arrived in Penang around 9.00am in the Morning. He can not return to his wife residence, as he is no more welcome, after the letter she wrote ordering him not to visit her or return to her abode. These separation was preplanned by Delilah Cold as Ice, so as to cause a Divorce between Esor and Otard. Otard then took a taxi to his parents house. He was like a stranger there. The feelings of a family relationship is no longer there. Otrad offered to pay his step-mother Nae RM50.00 a month for rental. Otard was free of his financial obligations as his wife don't want him anymore. He decided to take a rest and stop working away from the pressure and stress he had been having. He never told his father what has happened in his life in Uk, or Bandar Sri Bagawan. He never disclosed the relationship with his wife either. Otard is a silent person, as they said, silence is golden.

Otard spent carefully what ever savings he had, living a quiet and peaceful life. He got rid of his books he had collected in his younger days. He took them to the second book shops and sold them. Therre was not much money in them, except he wanted them to be in good hands. He found out in his thoughts that his step mother was Mandy Amanda the Assistant Housekeeper at Flemings Hotel. As she comes home from market she would cried to Otard father she misplaced her keys and could not find them. The key was symbolic to a phallaus in Otard's thoughts. In other words, she want sex with Otard with Mandy Amanda.

Otard took notice of the incident, as to him it was just a coincidence. He the spent his time going down town window shopping. He saw a few movies in town attracted his attention. The movie were, "Deadly Sorcery" "Deadly Red Chant" the Alchemist" and "Practical Magic" and "Witchcraft 5". He went to see Deadly Sorcery at Dalit Cinema, and was shocked to find his thoughts of Bolton all returned in the film and he was suffering continuous call of nature while at the cinema watching the film. Even in his call of nature, he could hear swear and bad words come out with the fecal oral mater through his rectum with the voice of Esor mother Hol. He spent most of the time in the toilet than watching the film. He begin to understand and get a rough idea of what was happening in Bolton.

A few days later, he went to watch another movie the Deadly Red Chant, and the same happened to him. He answer the called of nature more than watched the film. He then understand how it all happened to him in Bolton and London again. Then a week later he watched Witchcraft 5. Nothing happens to him, but he could hear them scolding him to have a sexual relationship with Delilah.He had enough of the occult, witchcraft and black magic. He did not watched the Alchmist nor Practical Magic.

Otard took his holiday in his parents house and have his rest. In the afternoon he stroll down town, and visit his friend Wohc at the Music Wonderland and past his time. He would be there till around 6.00pm then walked home. The Music Wonderland was around walking distance to his parents house. He came to know Wohc after buying some musical cassette. There then they develop their friendship.

They would sit and talk to past the time. At times, he would visit his school mate from Georgetown Secondary at the Penang Radio Shop. They would drink coffee and talk, though he purchased noting from him, and his school mate became furious.

Otard's father would listen to some Thai Prayers morning and evening. He would then go for his Mahjong session at the nearby coffee shop. He would return late at night, not joining Otard and or Otard step-mother for dinner. Otard father have an enormous collection of Thai talisman and amulets. He would devote his time to his collections and Mahjong. Otard would never understand why he wanted so much talisman and amulets. Some believers would visit Otard's father Rovivrus and asked for blessing, guidance and talisman or amulets. Perhaps that is why he kept a vast amount of Thai talismans and amoulets.

Otard's father received a mail from Esor Lawyer, informing him that his son marriage to Esor had broken down beyond reconciliation and Esor seeks divorce. In the letter Esor Lawyer wrote Esor had lost contacted with Otard. One strange part of the letter wrote the lawyer was that the lawyer said that Otard father had lost contacted of his husband Otard, who is the son of Rovivrus. Otard did not see the mistake of the divorce letter till after the divorce. It was all a mind game till they got the word order right. On receiving the letter Otard mind was disturbed and could not think of what action to take. This was heart break number one.

After many months, Otard decided to go back to England to make earn some money before settling down in Malaysia and also to divorce his wife. As Otard was not well versed in Bahasa Malaysia, his only employment opportunity is UK. Before his journey back to UK he planned to give his bed room to his step-sister Acirtap. He need a work permit no more, as he is now a permanent resident in UK. When he was in UK and befriended Mil, he visited his house a number of times. Mil own a trunk in his hall where he kept his things. This inspired Otard to purchase one such trunk before departing for UK. He sent the trunk to UK prior to his visit to UK at the addressed he corresponded with for the bed and breakfast. He planned to stay on his arrival in UK at the bed and breakfast in Queeens Mansion. Otard purchase a book at the local book shop, for his step sister Acirtap. The title was Macbeth.

That evening before catching his flight to UK, Otard had dinner with his father, step-mother and step sister. They had "Hor Fun" and rice with some meat and vegetable dishes. His brother-in-law Eeb took him to the bus station. From there he caught a bus to the capital, Kuala Lumpur. This time his second elder sister assisted him. She purchased him an Aeroflot air ticket to London. Before leaving for London, he visited his sister Ynnej. He stayed over at her residence for two days and night. The next day they went to air port, for him to catch the flight to London. Otard Luggage was over loaded and had to pay for excess weight. Otard finally got the problem settled with the help of his sister Ynnej.

Chapter 14

Returned to UK

Prior to returned to UK, Otard had book a room at the bed and breakfast at the Queen Maison, in Hampstead, London. He arrived in Heathrow airprt and took the tube to the bed and breakfast. It was already evening, so he took his rest after he went out for dinner. In the morning he searched for a room to let. He found one in 1 Cedar Grove. The land lady was Melanka Rristovich a Yugoslavian woman. She was a very big size woman of enormous built. She charged Otard 80 pounds British Sterling a month He moved into Cedar Grove. By the way the trunk had arrived and he took it to Esor friend's house in Plashet Road and store it there as there was no place in the room he rented in Cedar Grove. The next day Otard sat out looking for a job. He found a job at Oliver's coffee shop. Otard father was the brain of Saint Xavier Naudine. Xavier Naudine who operate the Oliver Coffee Shop was the owner. Terry Satchwill was the master baker there. He was the brain of Otard so is Saint Xavier Naudine. Xavier Naudine would say while Otard was serving the customer and preparing the food, like "that would do, much, much too much". Terry Satchwill would work in Otard Brain, serving "Next please, or Who is Next, How can I help you?" Returning home to his rented room at 1 Cedar Grove he had a tough time cleaning up the bath so he can use as the landlady would shave her legs and leave her hair all over the bath tub.

Otard would work late and come home with some bread for her from Oliver. The pay was low only 60 pounds a month. The supervisor Jane Brownoki mistreated him badly and bully him a lot. He never got a proper lunch or tea break. Otard left the job in Oliver and took a part time work at Quality Inn Leicester Square as a Grill Chef. Mr Irani was the manager there. Mr Irani was the puppet master I mentioned earlier. Quality Inn has 7 people working. They Roy Santos, Mia, Guna seleen, Babaos, Raja Krisna and Ray Lego. In the interview he asked Otard to cooked him an omelet, which Otard did that's how he got the job.

Some thing strange happened. He found his 3 dimensional body flatten making him feel like two dimensional. H does not know what action to take to get well, but to remain feeling two dimensional. His thoughts tell him, he is clipped between a glass and a picture in a picture frame. He now has a questioned is where is the picture frame that clipped him in that make him feel two dimensional. He then carried on as normal as he can, else what other choice have he.

Milanka would send thoughts to Otard scolding him for not loving her. One day Otard got fed up with the scolding and approach her and declare his love for her. She Scoffed at Otard and laughed at him. The next day the rental increase. She said in Otardd mind, "you wanted me so the rent must increase". Otard went and lodge a complain to the social services. She got very angry so she terminate Otard rental and Otard have to move out.

Otard than founded a room in 2 Montpelier Road owned by an Irish lady Anne Veronica Rafferty. She charged him 160.00 pound per month. Otard did two jobs to be able to pay for the rental. Besides maintaining his job at Quality Inn, he did another job at Commercial Catering Company, serving school meals. The Boss at Commercial Catering Group was Judy Cannon and Pat Richardson. By this time Otard had rented the room at 2 Montpelier road and had collected his trunk, and had brought it with him.

After working in the school meals for a month or two, Otard was transferred to work in the production outlet. The Supervisor was Brenda Mosin, Magret William and Veronica Hammond. The manager at the production outlet was Alan Jenkins. After working for a few weeks at the production outlet Otard lost his Samsosnite Side Pack containing his driving license, and some 50 pounds sterling's. Veronican Hammond was a Jamician woman, and Otard believes she took the Samsonite Side Pack. Otard believes shed practice Voodoo. On losing the bag Otard found Otard soul was being sliced at the catering plant. In Voodoo, you have to steal something from the victim before you can cause him harm.

Otard was injured and found the knife cutting him and could not work any more. Otard went to see a doctor a Dr M. G. U. Mia the local General Practitioner. He prescribed some medicine for him. He find it difficult to work at the production unit, as he had become fearful of the knife the excel slicer. With his sickness, Otard stayed at his rental room, in 2 Montpelier Road. Otard found the books and printed materials he brought with him from Malaysia began to talk in his mind. This made Otard feel crazy.

The Divorce of Otard and Esor came to take place on the 24th September 1986 at the Bow County Court at 10.15 am for the pronouncement of a decree. On that day morning, Otard woke up like any normal day. He then picked up thoughts scolding him from Esor parents. They were using terrible bad words scolding Otard. After the divorce they still continue to scold Otard. This was his heartache number one. While all this was happening, the puppet master of Otard Mr Irani manipulate to removal of President Ferdinand Marcos of Philippines. President Marcos was a puppet of Het. This happened throughout the world, removing all Het puppets, and replacing with Mrr Irani puppets.

Then Otard remembered the drawings he had that made him God at Flemings Hotel and the burning and destruction of his home in Upton Park, tells him that this printed materials and drawings in the paper would substitute for the paper works he had drawn, and started pasting them in the trunk. His friend Mil, once told him, he kept all that is wanted in the the trunk, and what he don't want and need outside the trunk and kept in the house. Since he was not working, he spent his time pasting in the trunk all his books. He tore up the pages and pasted them in. He then went to purchased more books and comics at the Atlantic Book Shop and Forbidden Planet. He pasted them in the trunk. He believes that the paper works would work on him like the way the drawing would on him while working at Flemings Hotel in the dangerous eighties. He is not drawing any more as the last time the drawings his mind fell on to the paper and he became possessed. He used the drawing drawn by the professionals artists in the comic books and these other books he bought.

He remembered how he did it in his younger days a his parents house that gets him what he wants. But this time it did not worked. It only create agro. His second elder sister Ynnej visited UK and paid him a visit at Montpelier street. He did not tell his sister what was wrong. After the paper works his mind still fell on to the bee hive next to the window to his room. The bees flew into attacked his room.

He had a hard time fighting the deadly invasion. He finally got rid of the bees, but the bees hive got into his brain. His brain begins to have a humming sound of the bees. Some weeks passed, he decided to return home to Penang, to try to get well as he was still jobless after the cut in his soul.

Otard found out too late that his paper works were all wrong. He got himself more enemies than friends. His bad luck came to him, and he get scolding where ever he went. To make matter worse, Otard was not allowed to bath more than once a day. The landlady Ann Veronica Rafferty reprimand Otard for taking his bath twice a day. Otard left for Penang, for a week holiday to recuperate himself. He was down and out.

He bought an Aeroflot ticket to Penang, via Kuala Lumpur. He arrived in Penang that morning, and took a taxi to his parent's house. He has no bed room anymore, as before he left, he gave up his bed room to his step-sister. He slept in the hall that night and the humming sound in his head keep blaring, making it impossible for him to sleep. As sleep won't come Otard opened the window and the sound disappear. When he closed the window the sound came back. He wondered what he should do with this in his life. He went to buy a safety boot as when he worked in the kitchen, he kept getting thoughts that the knife in the kitchen would fell on his foot and cut off his toes.

There was not much to do as Otard was jobless after the knife incident that cause him sickness while working at Commercial Catering Group. Otard was in Penang, for only a couple of days. The morning, before leaving for United Kingdom, Otard bought a tortoise bun and some flour cake and a tin of Cow and Gate condensed Milk. He spread the condensed milk on the tortoise bun and eat. During the stay at his parents house, over the past few days Otard pick up thoughts that Otard step-mother and in the early eighties, his step sister have no brain, so Otard left some of the tortoise bun and Cow and Gate condensed milk and some flour cakes for them to eat so as to passed on his brain to them. Otard did not know that his brain he left behind for them contain the following persons from Sheraton Utama Hotel at Bandar Sri Bagawan, was Kilali bin Mohamed Dawood, Abdul whaid, Sapari Labaja and Tony Anbutang Paluti, and of course Idris Ismail. Otard has no idea this would give thoughts to his step mother thinking Otard brain is malay and Otard would be under psychic attack by his step-mother as she sis a chinese jew.

That morning Otard left for the bus station, in Komtar. He took a trishaw to Komtar to catch a Consortium bus to Kuala Lumpur. Otard had problems with his boots. It seems his foot seems to get bigger by the minutes and his foot is crammed and painful. From there Otard took his bus to Kuala Lumpur. There he caught a taxi to Subang Airport and there he caught a flight to UK. In returning to UK he encountered his land lady Ann Veronica Rafferty with more problems. This time, she screamed at Otard with bad words and accused Otard of being a drug addict knowing full well, Otard never drink, smoke or touch drugs. Otard thought of suing her for malicious slander. She then evicted Otard from his rental room. He gave Otard one week notice to quit his accommodated rental. Once again, Otard have to move to find accommodation.

Now Otard was desperate for a job and a room to let. He found a room at 75 The Avenue, an illegal bed and breakfast. The landlady Sue Scarmen has no Bed and Breakfast license. She provide bread and coffee for breakfast at Do it yourself. She was a very big size woman. She and her friend Eve runs the Bread and Breakfast. Before Otard move into the Bed And Breakfast, Sue Scarmen request Otard to kneel down and worshiped her.

Otard then found a job at the Granville Harvester in Elaing Broadway. There he was to work as a catering Assistant. Otard had given up the idea of management work, as it was all an abused of Aliens, to get work done for a low pay. He had been under paid and over worked in the past at Empire Ballroom, Flemings hotel, etc.

At Granville Harvester at first he worked with Paul Ervin as the head chef and his sister the assistant chef. They were Irani puppets. When working with Paul Erwin, he Paul Erwin would sent out thoughts that Otard is himself the chef cooking and he is Otard in the kitchen preparing and washing up. He would then sent out thoughts to Otardd to steal the meat cut left over to eat at the chopping board where he was working and in the thoughts, if Otard so dare as to put his fingers to steal the meat, will get his fingers chopped off. One strange thing is that after cooking and at the end of the evening, Paul Erwin would cuddled up and tremor all over.

The manager at that time was John comings. They were running the place for a few months before being transferred to another outlet and was replaced by Gordon Mcloud, and the chef William Lim Kegan, Eugene. These is Het puppets. There is two Eugene, the other was Eugene O'Neil. The waitress was Jane, Margret, and the waiter Peter, and Collin Key. This time Otard old puppet master Het, was in full charge. Gordon Mcloud was his puppet. Otard work with them in the afternoon shift. In the kitchen as catering assistant, he worked with an Indian Lady named Prem. In the adjoining next room is the pub. Eugene O'Neil was the bar tender. He works with Ean Smith.

The condition then was much better. No body bothered Otard as he worked though he picked up thoughts scolding him throughout the working hours in the kitchen. One day while working in the kitchen with a national from the same country as him, a grievance broke out. It wass a misunderstanding about space. That boy with the same nationality as him though belong to another race wanted to occupy all the space and Otard have no space to prepare the food. Otard was furious, and walked out of the kitchen and left the job and headed for home. Otard had given up in working in UK. He was planning to go home. Any way, throughout his stay in UK since he returned, his thoughts is being scolded all the time by Old Man Kee who is also Het his neighbor in Penang next to his parents home evicting him from his home ordering him to returned to Malaysia.

He found that the friendly atmosphere he enjoyed the last time he was in England in the 1970's were gone. He was waiting to sort out the things and have enough money to go home to Malaysia. He was dammed scared of the land lady Sue Scarmen, as she would come by from time to time and scold him. Otard continue with his paper work to work out things right for him. It seems all his paper works is no avail. By this time the brain of Mr Gaoul Hati had entered Otard brain. "It is saying are you Mad, I am Mad." It was the work of Mad Ying whoes fathe by thee name "How many years you been Mad".

A few days later the Manager Gordon Mcloud came by his rental room and called on Otard to return to work. He said he sympathies with Otard and understand the grievance between the boy and Otard, as is a common racial problems he suffered from his country of origin. Otard continue to work as he the boy bothered him no more. After two months Otard gave in his resignation, as he had saved enough to buy an air fare to return to Malaysia.

Chapter 15

Returned to the East

Prior to returning to the East from Europe in UK, to Malaysia, his land lady Sue Scarmen gave him a white suit to wear. He left for the house early in the morning at 6.00 am to catch the morning tube to Heathrow airport. He caught the Aeroflot flight at the Heathrow airport with no hassle. He reached Penang at 12.20 am.

He saw a piece of red paper on the ground, and his thoughts told him his father had passed away. And the funeral had taken place. He called on the door and knocked and knocked but to no avail. There are two reason to this version of not opening the door. As Otard father lies in the wake, with him is a full white suit and I wore a full white suit resembles his father returned. Another version is a Bruce Lee movie of Chen Zen returning in white suit at the death of his Master in the Movie Fist of Fury. Finally at 1.30am they opened the door. His second sister Ynnej and his steep mother Nae opened the door and let him in. They broke the news to him, about the death of his father and the funeral took place yesterday. He never told them, he knew all about it.

Otard was lost for words. Otard second sister Ynnej then mentioned she had paid all the bills of Otard's father funeral expenses. They then gave Otard some Nonya cakes used for praying the day before morning during the funeral, and a cup of Milo then went to bed. Otard slept of the deck chair on the hall. The next day, they are going to collect the ashes of his father at the Crematorium at Batu Gantung.

One thing strange at the ceremony they called his younger brother Hendrix as big brother to carried his father ashes to the Columbarium. In Otard thoughts they have sealed Otard in his father coffin and had him creamated. The Malay boy one of the puppet of Irani, Kilali Bin Mohamed Dawood said in malay "Abang balek Kampung, tanam Jagong" meaning Otard is planted in the soil. After the Columbarium Service at the Thai Temple, Otard big sister told Otard She is taking him to see a Psychiatrist. She mention the Psychiatrist is a friend Halludba our cousin. He was a Dr Tan Chee Kwan at Lam Wah Ee Hospital Penang. He is the best there is compared to another a Singh at the University Hospital University in Kuala Lumpur.

Otard and his sister went to see the Psychiatrist Dr Tan at the Lam Wah Ee Hospital. Dr Tan said he is suffering from schizophrenia and gave his an injection, and some tablets to take. He gave him a book "Heal Your Sick Mind" which his sister took and kept. They went home, and Otard hand starts to tremor. As he had given up his abode at his parents house, his sister-in-law help his find a room at Maxwell Road where she was staying. In Otard mind Otard can hear his first Uncle the Big White One, saying Otard is a danger to the elders in the family, as he is the youngest, and must be confine to a mental sanatorium. The New puppet Master Mr Irani, have reshuffle the family tree, and made Otard who is the eldest into the youngest. Otard was at lost and not know who he could turn to solve these problems. He is in a messes situation. The new puppet master has made him into a women in the Dallas movie.

He made Otard into Sue Ellen, and so is his sisters, and they become Mad and suffers the same fate. Sue Ellen was the wife of the notorious JR in the Movie Dallas. Halludba was JR all the time. Otard youngest brother Hendrix was enjoying the luxury and comfort of a loving, passion sex life as a big brother. They made it in movie land as the guy who played the notorious JR played Major Anthony Nelson in the movie "I dreamed of Jennie" and Hendrix and his wife enjoyed the benefit of the show. Hendrix would called his wife Dar, who is Ioo and Ioo in returned would called Otard youngest brother Hendrix Dar. The actor of the film was Larry Hackman. Halludba and Hendrix share the same name, Egg Yolk. It was Halludba Egg Yolk, and Hendrix Egg Yolk.

Otard was branded Mad, and a Schizophrenic. With the essential tremor and a medical record for schizophrenia how is he going to find a job wondered Otard. Otard looked around. Finally He got a job at Super Komtar as security guard with a salary of RM300.00 on 1st June 1990. It was a routine job, guarding Super Komtar performing manual duties. After working there for a while he befriended a friend Kok Poon. Then he met Naej the Bullet. They became good friends. Kok Poon and a friend Lim, together with Otard, they would go swimming in Telok Bahang. One day, he cconfessed to Kok Poon, that his ancestry was linked to the great Ayatollah Ruhollah Khomeini. He did not know what made him said that, which he regret later in his days. Later in his days he found out it was Kok Pooh paper work and was his paper work and was his thoughts projections that made him said what he had said. Otard said all that was in Kok Poon Mind. It was his friend Naej, that showed him how all this was done, as she was the Bullet, and all Brewster passed through her before attacking. There were good friends and there were bad friends. Friends from the survivors of the Kingdom of Christ under Kee or Het and not so good friends form Irani Kingdom. He then left Super Komtar to work with Pamn Enterprise selling hand phones in 1995. Otard was with Super Komtar for 5 years, as security gurad.

It was a pity for Otard, as the accommodation he had is being reclaimed by the developer and is on the way to demolition to make way for a Mall. Otard had to move a again. His sister arranged for him to rent a room at his step-mother house. Finally they converted the verandah and open space by the air well for Otard to reside in. On moving to his step-mother house he lost his relationship with his friend Naej. They were very closed together and were good friends. She visited him daily, when he was residing with his sister-in law. She do not like to visit his steep mother house, so she decide to leave for Kuala Lumpur. This was heart break number three. Otard suffered his heartache by the umbers. He always thought of Naej, as she would come every morning clean up his room, wash his clothes and make him a hot soup in the slow cooker. She would then visit him in the evening, then they go out, to the movies or just to the supermarket.

Before he change job, he applied for a government low cost housing. Finally after a few years he received a reply for a housing project in Paya Terubong and to deposit some money for down payement. These came about after the accommodation he stays at Maxwell Road, was to demolish to make way for a shopping Mall. Otard then decided to change job and work as a promoter for Pamn Enterprise selling hand phones. Otard was stationed at Butterworth and he stayed at the company hostel sharing a room with 4 people. In Pamn Enterprise,he lived in a hostel in

Butterworth. One thing strange is that each morning as he report for work, his boss Jack would command in Otards thoughts to go to sleep and Otard automatically fell sleepy. Otard was thinking how to work like that. So Otard decided to leave the job, after some months.

The pay was very low so Otard worked for almost a year. Otard find this job boring, and not to his liking, so he changed jobs. At this time, Otard purchase a Malaysian made car Kanchil. To Otard this was a boring job and too much technicalities involved. He left in 1996 to join Enersave Engineering system Sdn Bhd. He decided to work for Enersave as a technician. His job is to maintained water filter plant at various factories in the Northern district of Penang. After doing filter plant maintenance for some months he was transferred to sewage plant maintenance in Northern district. Otard looses interest in the job as it sewage removal was a tough and terrible job. The pay was horrible. He was only earning around ringgit eight hundred a month only.

After this he was video Acarde attendant at Penang Swimming Club. There he met Tenaj. They became good fiends. She was staying at the same flat as himself Otard. She stayed on the 11th floorf and Otard stayed on the 16th floor. She was a divorcee with two daughters and one son. Otard left the job after a few months of working as the job offer no prospect. In 1997 he joined TT water Theme Park Sdn Bhd as a full time Supervisor. He then went back to be in house security at the Dutch Baby factory complex at the capital in Kuala Lumpur. It was a private firm managing security together with Dutch Baby own security patrolling the place reason for this is because of company Insurance there must be two security. One from a private security contractor and one from its internal security. The pay wasn't that good, as he got to pay rental for his room even he stays in his brother house. And the job was long twelve hours. From 7 am to 7pm and from 7pm to 7am. The he place of working was too far so in a few month after working he resigned. He went to study for the Maslaysian Insurance Institute Exam and passed. He then went to sell Insurance. He did not do well as he has no network of friends. He then went to worked as a driver for Telehep Services Sdn Bhd for 8 years.

All this time he was still under psychic attack and mental poisoning. The attacked came from the west. This was too much and it angered the puppet master of Otard a lot. Otard thoughts tell him to paste a japaness flag on his vision frame, and so he did. The agro was coming from the west, Europe, Uk and America. Even though Ayotolah Ruhulloh Kommeni were managing America and the west, after the Iranian Embassy Siege, they have to answer to their master. Irani was the puppet master but he still have a master behind him. This was Ah Tan. Ah Tan was angered with the attacked on Otard effecting the whole of Asia by thoughts from the West under the rule of Ayotalah. He discussed with his counter parts in Japan and drew their plans. Osama Bin Laden was chosen for the jobs. They aimed to down the tower of Babel as in the Old Testament.

On September 11, 2001, 19 militants associated with Islamic Extremist group al-Quaeda hijacked four airlines and carried out suicide attacks against target in the United States. Two of the planes were flown into the towers of the World Trade Center in New York City, a third plane hit the Pentagon just outside Washington, DC., and the fourth plane crashed in Pennsylvania. Often referred to as 9/11, the attack resulted in extensive death and destruction, triggering major U.S. initiatives to combat terrorism and defining the presidency of George Bush. Over 3,000 people were killed during the attacks in New York City and Washington, D.C., including more than 400 police officers and firefighters.

Ah Tan the puppet master was furious with the way the great Ayatollah Ruhollah Khomeini was running the West. Ayatollah Ruhollah Khomeini did not know that his puppet master reside in the east, and he has no right what so ever to mental poisoning the thoughts of the east and launching Psychic attacks. It was Ayatollah Ruhollah Khomeini America after the American Embassy Siege. Ayatollah as a puppet master running America came to a lost as there was no more brain after the attack. It was like using fire to fight fire. This woke up the Americans, the sleeping giant. It took some time before the Americans regain their senses.

Mr Irani retilated and his puppet did his bidding in America and America went to war in Afghanistan. The US puts pressure on Taliban the ruling power of Afghanistan were accused by the US of protecting Osama Bin Laden. Taliban requests for negotiations with the US were rejected in favor of military action, and 7th October 2001 US- led Operation Enduring Freedom began in Afghanistan. The aim of Operation Enduring Freedom was to find Osama Bin Laden, remove the Taliban from power, and prevent the use of Afghanistan as a Terrorist Heaven. The US was supported by broad collation of international forces including Afghan Northern Alliance, United Kingdom and Canada.

Kabul fell to collation forces on 13th October 2001. In early Deccember fierce fighting took place near the Tora Bora caves, where Taliban leader Mullah Omar and Osama Bin Laden were believe to be. Both men evaded capture and went into hiding. Kandahar, thee last major Taliban stronghold, fell on 7th Decemeber 2001, making the end of Taliban's rule in Afghanistan. There were excluded from Bonn Agreement that formed a draft constitution for Afghanistan, and in 2004 Hamid Karzai was elected country's president.

Otard continue building his paper work his vision wall, or you call it vision chart or vision frame. He believe this had worked for him in his childhood days, surely this will worked now. He changed his job as according to the wishes of his puppet master. He then seek employment as Aassistant Building Supervisor with Key Building System Sdn Bhd. He did not find the job he wanted but found a desire form the job to be a Property Negotiator. So he left the job and becoming a building Supervisor for Key Building System at Taman Krystal at Mount Erskine to become a Proeprty Negotiator. He then paid for a training course at New Bob and took up training. On completion training he became a Property Negotiator. This job he liked a lot, though he don't have the Network of buyers or sellers, landlords or tenants. But, he was able to Negotiate some deals and was able to work to his 62 years of age, and called his quit.

He then went to worked as a transporter for Yamaha fetching the admin staffs to and from work. The time was flexible, that is how he was able to have ample time tell this story. With his free time he was able to rebuild his brain damage in the burning in the house in UK at Upton Park Road. As Delilah had been a problem to him, he pasted a brain with vast amount of agro as to get of the passion curse and love curse and it worked. The loved he felt for Delilah came to an end.

He truly missed his wife and children and wished they would returned to him. He visualize and build vision chart to fulfill this dream. He truly hoped one day they will return. To overcome the madness for Delilah as cold as ice, the daughter of darkness, he fixed his gaze on his family and loved ones, including friends. He began a new hobby of passion, building picture frames, of his friends, family, and loved ones. He believes that what you see in front of your eyes is what you get. He believes that seeing his family, loved ones and friends, he will meet them where ever he goes, and have a happy life.

He build picture frames of his name, and surname. He saw this in his friend house, that is in his hall is his name, so he followed and build his name in his flat. He build names of his sister and parents. Now he has accomplished all this he has a piece of mind. He had gotten rid of the love curse and passion curse for Delilah. He now have a quiet life and wait for his family to return if the paper work is correctly done.

Otard conclusion, his definition of God, is there is no God. It is all in the Mind, the brain works in the mind, and the people are the part and parcel of the mind in the brain that called God. God is man make, and men control the happenings of the world. Those who are superior in thinking, are dominate the weaker, and the weaker is a puppet to the stronger will, who becomes the puppet master.

Thinking, is created by vision charts, dream charts, or vision wall, vision frames, scrap books, vision albums, etc. these projects the thoughts, of motivated men and women, takings them to heights of success. What you paste is what you get, and what you see in front of your eyes is what is in your head, in your brain, and in your mind. How it comes to work in wonders, is the mind accept the pictures in front of him or her, and the brain absorb it, and deliver it to the subconscious and the unconscious. All people men or women share the same mind, is a plane of twilight zone, where anything can exist, in the outer limit. By taking one step beyond, we can tap on the mind and manipulate others, control events, and move the world in different trend of thoughts.

Otard gave up his position and surrender it to Mr Irani the New Puppet Master. These is why we have world events taking place, as the imagination of Mr Irani to fulfill his dream of a new Millennium for his children and people, his followers and believers. They wanted to enjoy what the Predecessor had before the Millennium, and to punish all who does him wrong in the past. He just wanted to do the opposite and he wants the puppets master earlier before his time, and their puppets to suffer the fate he suffers. The Buddhist called this Karma, even the good can be bad to him in his days, and now he is in power, the good is him and the bad is the good people of the past, during the reign of their puppet master. Like the fall of the Shah and President Marcos. It is the other side of the coin.

Otard was classified a Jew by Mr Irani and his puppets, especially Kelali Bin Mohamed Dawood who launched psychic attack and mental poisoning on Otardd, after he bought the Holy Kabalah, when he was residing in UK before the burning. To-day they still attacked him. All Otard can do now is to change their trend of thoughts with his vision frames. He hope to win this time. Otard had a hard life. The Jew also attacked him in their puppet Kok Gnep. Otard finally find out through his new paper work that it was Kok Genp who wore him to destroy his home in London, England. The brain that burn the properties In London is Romy, the guy he worked with in Tartino coffee Shop, England. Otard now knows the truth behind all this, and hope his family and friends with his new paper works will understands the situation, and make up their relationship.

Printed in the United States
By Bookmasters